I'd know those eyes anywhere

She couldn't wait for an ambulance.

Gently, Alice turned over the body of the man struck by a car. Even as she probed the gash on his head, she couldn't help but notice the silken texture of his raven hair, or that his face was devastatingly handsome. He suddenly groaned, his lush lips parting, his thick jet eyelashes fluttering. And then he opened his eyes.

For the second time that day, everything in Alice stilled.

She'd never seen this man. But she knew the eyes. They belonged to a man accused of murder. A man she loved. A man whose voice she'd only thought she'd heard tonight. It was this man whose disappearance had filled her heart with so much terror— and whose reappearance now filled her eyes with tears.

"Dylan," she gasped. "My God, it's Dylan."

ABOUT THE AUTHOR

In 1993 Jule McBride's dream came true with the publication of her debut novel, *Wild Card Wedding*. It received the *Romantic Times* Reviewer's Choice Award for Best First Series Romance. Ever since, the author has continued to pen stories that have met with strong reviews and made repeated appearances on romance bestseller lists.

Books by Jule McBride

The Strong, Silent Type

Jule McBride

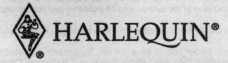

HARLEQUIN®

TORONTO • NEW YORK • LONDON
AMSTERDAM • PARIS • SYDNEY • HAMBURG
STOCKHOLM • ATHENS • TOKYO • MILAN • MADRID
PRAGUE • WARSAW • BUDAPEST • AUCKLAND

ISBN 0-373-22519-9

THE STRONG, SILENT TYPE

Copyright © 1999 by Julianne Randolph Moore

This edition published by arrangement with Harlequin Books S.A.

® and TM are trademarks of the publisher. Trademarks indicated with ® are registered in the United States Patent and Trademark Office, the Canadian Trade Marks Office and in other countries.

Visit us at www.romance.net

Printed in U.S.A.

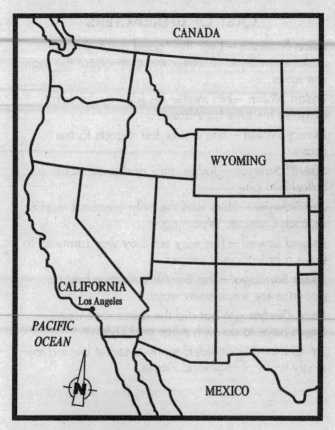

WESTERN UNITED STATES

CAST OF CHARACTERS

Alice Eastman — Ever the "good girl," she will make enemies to discover the truth about the man she loves.

Dylan Nolan — No matter his identity, he can't disguise his love for Alice.

Nancy Nolan — She'd take her secrets to the grave.

Sheriff Sawyer — Judge, jury and executioner all rolled into one.

Jan Sawyer — Hers was the only unsolved murder in Rock Canyon, Wyoming.

Leland Lowell — The wiry cowboy was rumored to have a hair-trigger temper.

Louie Santiago — The Bel-Air detective had no patience for small-town ways.

Lang Devlyn — What did the aged rock icon's death have to do with Alice and Dylan?

Dr. Clark — He shielded many a secret behind the costly walls of Highland Home.

Prologue

Oleander, cinders and wet leaves.

With the unexpected scents came a rush of queasiness, a feeling of suffocation, and Dylan Nolan stilled his steps, tilted his head and listened over the sound of his hammering heart for...

For...

He wasn't sure what.

Sometimes, when he was herding cattle in the mountains, he got this same feeling, as if a predator had been watching him a long time, waiting for the right second to pounce. Later, he'd usually discover bear or bobcat tracks on the trails. Now he simply paused, feeling uncomfortably conscious of his new jeans' scratchy denim, the confining pull of his sports coat and the pinch of stiff black goatskin ropers; they were so unlike his broken-in work shoes, with their supple leather that molded his feet like gloves.

Swallowing hard, he kept his eyes watchful and tried to shake off the uneasy feeling, but the quiet church hallway, with its connecting auditorium and public rooms had definitely unnerved him. It was sud-

denly *too* quiet. Eerie. Hard to believe his and Alice's
wedding reception was in full swing so close by.

Just a dang case of nerves, Dylan assured himself,
taking in the vague outline of the door to the choir's
robing room. Hell, any cowboy'd feel jittery on his
wedding day, right?

But the feeling lingered. Dylan had just changed
into traveling clothes and had been racing toward the
reception, anxious to get started on his and Alice's
honeymoon. Now he tightened a finger around the
hanger that held his tux, letting the long transparent
plastic dry-cleaning bag trail behind him. Suddenly
the plastic fluttered. Had something moved? Was
somebody in the choir room? Dylan listened past the
sound of plastic, waiting for…

For…

Something *bad* to happen.

For a second, he smelled something more elusively
disturbing in the air than the oleander. Something me-
tallic. Minerals or sulfur, maybe.

Blood.

Hairs rose on his nape.

But no, there was only…an odd feeling of déjà vu.
And what might have been a memory. Dylan envi-
sioned a lawn, sloping to a lake rimmed by mud-
caked leaves and poisonous white-flowering oleander
bushes. There was a swing set facing the lake, and
hanging from chain hooks, two empty swings blew
back and forth over the grass. In his mind's eye, Dylan watched them move until he could almost hear
the soft, protesting groans of the unoiled chains.

For years, this place—the lake, the swing set, the

oleander—had appeared in his dreams and nightmares. But was it real? And if so, why couldn't Dylan ever recall where exactly he'd seen it? Or when?

Even after the scent of oleander vanished, replaced by wood polish and fresh spring air, Dylan didn't want to move. Dammit, why was the placid lake scene he'd remembered so strangely menacing? And why would he recollect it on his wedding day? Why, at this particular moment? Was it because…

Because…

The memory still eluded him.

Shrugging, Dylan shifted the tux hanger on his shoulder and started walking again. To take his mind off the unsettling thoughts, he checked his inner sports-coat pocket. "Plane tickets to Hawaii," he murmured. "Cash, credit card…" After a moment, a fledgling smile tugged at his lips. Boy, his new father-in-law would kick Dylan's sorry butt if he forgot something.

So would Dylan's mom.

And his bride.

The thought of Alice with her fine blond hair and grass-green eyes chased away any remaining demons. This afternoon, while Alice had calmly taken her wedding vows, she'd looked as untroubled as she had ten years ago when Dylan had first met her. Difference was, they weren't teenagers anymore. They were grown now.

And she was his wife.

Not that the honeymoon could begin for a few more hours. Hell, before they left the truck in the airport's long-term lot, they'd have to wash it. Too bad shaving cream would ruin the Ford's paint job, because the Just Married sign filled Dylan with so much pride he'd just as soon leave it. He didn't mind the spurs and beer cans tied to his bumper, either. They were a testament to the most important thing in his life—his love for Alice.

"I can't believe it," he muttered. What had come over him a minute ago? He was such a worrier! He had been, ever since he was a kid. This was the best day of his life, which didn't necessarily mean something bad was bound to happen. Why was he always waiting for the other shoe to drop?

At least Alice wasn't that way.

No, there wasn't a hint of darkness in Alice Eastman, no shadows or moodiness. She was tremendously positive, which was only one of a thousand reasons Dylan loved her. Now he silently vowed, come hell or high water, he'd never bring her a speck of trouble. Ever since he was a teenager, he'd lived for the sound of her soft voice, and more recently, for the quiet precious moments they shared, the naked cuddling and whispers...

Suddenly, his heart stuttered. There it was again! That infernal smell. Was someone here? Behind him?

Spinning around, Dylan gasped, "Who's—"

But he didn't finish. Swiftly, an unseen hand was thrust from the darkness, lifted the dry-cleaning bag and flung the plastic over Dylan's head like a hood. A hard male body slammed against Dylan's back, just as strong fingers clamped around his neck, holding the plastic tight and grasping the gold chain Dylan wore. The hand looped the chain, tightening it so it cut into Dylan's flesh, stealing his breath. For a confused second, Dylan thought he was drowning in the menacing lake from his dreams. *No, oh, no. It can't be.*

But it was. Everything went black.

Coming to, Dylan clawed at the man's hands, at the plastic against his face. *Don't take the medallion,* he wanted to say; the masculine smooth gold locket on the chain was a gift from Alice and it held her picture. But Dylan couldn't speak; wheezing breath was suctioning the plastic bag against his lips, pulling plastic into his mouth. He gagged. He had to fight! To hurt this guy! Kill him! But the fingers of his attacker sank deeper, pressuring Dylan's larynx while the man's lips settled on Dylan's plastic-covered ear.

"Leave now or she dies."

Who dies? Who dies? Tell me who!

But no words came, just more breath that pulled plastic deeper into Dylan's mouth and brought moisture into the bag, making it fog. *Don't shut your eyes. Don't ever shut your eyes. Keep them open or you'll die!* Behind that, came another more horrifying thought. *Oh, God, he's got a knife.*

A razor-sharp blade wiggled against the plastic, flicking at the artery in Dylan's neck. What was happening? Who would attack him in a church on his wedding day? Whose lips were pressed against his ear? Dylan strained to hear the sick, droning voice.

"Prom night...when you got a call your mother was in the hospital in River Run? Remember how you ran out the door and couldn't take Alice to the prom?"

There was something so familiar about the man's voice. Where had Dylan heard it? His mind raced, but now to the prom. It had been seven years ago when the official-sounding phone call sent him fleeing to his mother's side. He'd been lied to. Told his mother was in a car accident, near death, and he'd rushed out...

As the man rambled, Dylan remembered other times. The hang-up calls. The call that made him miss a football game that cost him his college scholarship... And with the recollections came the sudden, horrifying realization that this attacker might have been stalking him for years. "What do you want from me?" Dylan managed to croak through the bag.

"To see you suffer." The strangling hand tightened, forcing blackness to cloud Dylan's mind again.

"...follow you all the days of your life," Dylan suddenly heard. "I'll make sure you're nothing. That you have nothing. That you come to nothing."

Dylan would never know what happened then. His mind snapped. Gave out. Maybe he simply passed out again, since he couldn't breathe. Suddenly, the medallion was wrenched from his neck and the knife was pressed harder to his skin.

Just as he went limp, Dylan felt the iron grip loosen, lowering him to the floor. And he heard the man say, "Don't talk to anybody. Don't take your truck. Walk out of this church. Right out of your life. If you don't, I'll kill that pretty little wife of yours. Cut her sweet flesh into ribbons. Cut her until she bleeds like a pig. And while her blood drains, innocent little Alice will think it's you who's killing her, Dylan Nolan. I'll make sure of that. Damn sure.''

A breath pulled the plastic into his mouth again, but with no oxygen. Consciousness faded. And then everything went black again.

Dylan felt the cold, hardwood floor against his cheek. How long had he been passed out? Was Alice still all right? Panic seized him. Everything had happened so fast; it didn't seem real. It was insane! He glanced around. The man was gone. So was the tux. And the plastic...

Had it really been pulled over his head, suffocating him? Reminding him of the lake in his dreams? Everything seemed so unreal, as if the attack was a nightmare. Or as if he'd dissociated from reality. Even now, he was plagued by that feeling of dislocation. He was here...and somehow *not* here. In the present...and yet elsewhere.

Walk out of your life or I'll kill her.

Had the man really said that? In the hallway, there was no evidence of what had just happened. Not even a remnant of the plastic bag. No knife on the floor. Half crawling, Dylan managed to rise, clutching at his aching throat.

What should I do? What should I do?

I'll kill that pretty little wife of yours....

Oh, God, no!

Blindly, Dylan staggered forward. He had to get out of here! He needed air! He could still smell what he had all his life, whenever terror filled him—poison oleander and burning leaves smoldering into ash.

And it *was* a memory! The scent wasn't just a figment of his imagination. Dylan knew that now. It was how he knew the attacker was serious about murdering Alice. Because now Dylan remembered the day he'd first noticed—really noticed—that cloying scent. He'd been a first-grader. And then, just like today, he'd been fighting, gasping for breath while a strong strangling hand was wrapped tightly around his neck.

Chapter One

Summer, 1986

Thirteen-year-old Alice Eastman would always remember the first time she spoke to Dylan Nolan. Like all the other locals on the main street of Rock Canyon, Wyoming, she was watching the beat-up old Chevy angle into a spot in front of the general store.

"Here she comes, so hush up," Alice's mother said to the three women crowding around the cash machine. "And, Alice, can you please hop down, honey?"

As Alice slid off the counter, the owner of the store, Val Spencer, turned to Alice's mother. "Are you crazy? You and your husband can't just offer that woman a job at the ranch and let her stay in one of your guest cabins. She's a stranger. Who knows where she and her son are really from? She told people she lost her ID cards, and I heard she still hasn't bothered to bring the boy's records to the high school."

"How can she?" said Ivory, a waitress from the

truck stop. "Everybody says she's on the run from the boy's father. Maybe Nancy Nolan's not even her real name."

Val shook her head worriedly. "You're on the money there, Ivory. What if she's running from some psychopath? I mean, she's gorgeous. Maybe she was living somewhere else and she attracted some stalker…"

"Don't be ridiculous," said Alice's mother reasonably. "And Nancy Nolan's not running from any husband. She told me her husband died years ago when her son was just a baby."

Ivory's eyes narrowed with suspicion. "If so, any money the man left her is long gone."

"Judging from that ancient Chevy she's driving," agreed Val. "But she looks rich, doesn't she? And her clothes are expensive. At least the older ones. Ernestine took an apple pie over to the rooming house where she's been staying with her son—you know, just to be social—and Ernestine said the labels in her coats are all from fancy Los Angeles stores."

Ivory gasped. "See. She *said* she was from Des Moines."

"Maybe she lived in Des Moines *and* Los Angeles," Alice's mother said in censure. "And you mean to tell me that Ernestine actually went through that poor woman's closet?"

Val nodded. "Well, yes. Don't you think it's strange that Nancy Nolan's car broke down here, and she just up and decides to stay? I heard she pawned a big diamond ring, too. Delmar Sorrell over at the pawnshop swore it was damn near two carats. That's how she paid the garage for fixing the transmission on that god-awful car. I just wonder if her husband—"

"I really don't think she lied about having one," interjected Alice's mother, sounding thoroughly exasperated. "Both her and her son claim the man died years ago."

"Well, I know," said Val with a frown. "It's just that…that…"

That Nancy Nolan wasn't the type of woman whom men left alone for very long. Even at thirteen, Alice Eastman knew that much. "She's only thirty-four," chimed in Alice, tossing a long, white-blond braid over her shoulder and absently running her tongue over her new braces. "At least that's what she says. All the cowhands at the rooming house are sniffing around her, but she's not interested."

Slowly, the women turned and stared at Alice. "Where on earth did you hear such a thing?" demanded her mother.

Alice blushed. "Around."

Val grinned. "Hmm. Well, I bet I know why you're so interested, Alice."

The women, including Alice's mother, tittered.

Alice ducked her head and edged toward the door, hoping to get a better look at Nancy Nolan's dreamy sixteen-year-old son, Dylan, while Ivory's voice lowered with concern. "I don't care what you say. I know you want to help the woman by giving her a job and a decent place to live. And she does seem nice. But it's dangerous. She and her son have an air of…of…"

"Trouble about them," murmured Val worriedly.

Alice watched Nancy Nolan shut the car door and head toward the store. She was slender and long-legged with thick, shoulder-length brown hair. Even her beat-up Chevy never stopped people from immediately noticing how much she resembled Jackie Kennedy. Despite the faded jeans and old plaid flannel shirts she wore, she moved as gracefully as a model, her hips swaying gently, her head turning from side to side as if she expected to find people staring at her, which they always were. There was such an aura of mystery and money surrounding her that even the most curious Rock Canyon residents couldn't bring themselves to ask too many questions.

Almost too glamorous to be anybody's mother, Alice decided. Nancy Nolan definitely seemed to have something to hide. But she had class, too, so whatever secrets she'd left behind, they probably wouldn't follow. Nor would she ever talk about them. Nancy Nolan was the type of woman who took her secrets to the grave.

"Hello, Ms. Nolan," Alice said as she came in.

"Hello, Alice."

Now or never. Her heart skipping a beat, Alice ducked through the screen door and headed along the boardwalk connecting the main street's stores. From the corner of her eye, she could see Dylan Nolan, sitting inside the rusted-out Chevy. His arm was propped in the open car window, and through it, Alice could hear oldies playing on the radio. She recognized the song—Sugarloaf's "Green-Eyed Lady"—because her mother always kept their kitchen radio tuned to the same station, Top Rock of the Seventies.

"Hey there, Alice Eastman."

Her heart pounded. Looking as nonchalant as she could, she headed toward the car just as Dylan's well-defined lips formed the words, "Green-eyed lady, lovely lady."

Because Alice had green eyes, she got the impression that Dylan was singing for her, and she blushed. "Uh, hi."

"You *are* Alice, right?" he said. "My mom just got a job working for your dad, so we're gonna be living on your ranch. Cool, huh?"

"Yeah." She couldn't believe he was talking to her. All the older girls were already in love with him. And who could blame them? Dylan had straight golden hair and liquid brown eyes that shouldn't have been remarkable, but somehow were. He was sexier than any guy in the teen magazines Alice devoured. Her heart was still hammering as she leaned in the car window. Suddenly, she squinted. "Hey, did anybody ever tell you you look like Lang Devlyn?"

Dylan's eyes sparked with recognition, as if he'd heard that a thousand times. "Yeah, but no one I could love."

Love?

Alice giggled. Sixteen-year-old boys were such come-ons! Just like Lang Devlyn. In his heyday, Devlyn had been the King of Cool. Like Marlon Brando and Jimmy Dean, he was the strong, silent type, dressed in black leather, and was always photographed with fast motorcycles—and faster women. A rock-and-roll icon in the fifties, he later became a wealthy record producer. Even now, Alice's mom would get gooey-eyed when his songs came on the radio.

Dylan was still smiling. "Is that all you want to ask me?"

No. Did she dare ask the rest? She rested her elbow on the window edge near his. "Well…" She paused, and then feeling bolder rushed on. "Everybody's talking about you and your mom.…"

"And?"

"And they say you might be on the run from something." Leaning closer, Alice wondered if the sudden shiver she felt was due to the rumors or to her proximity to Dylan. Her voice hitched with apprehension. "Are you?"

"Nope." Dylan's irresistible smile deepened, showing a quick flash of straight white teeth, but Alice also noticed a dark shadow in his eyes—one so deep it made her shudder again despite the summer air. He continued, "But hey, maybe that's why I remind you of Lang Devlyn."

Alice squinted. "Why's that?"

"The element of mystery."

"Hmm." The darkness in his eyes vanished, and she managed a flirtatious laugh, feeling self-conscious. *Figures,* she thought, *I would get braces the week before meeting Dylan Nolan.* "So, you're a guy with a past, huh?"

"Or a future." He shot her an easy grin. "Who knows? Maybe I'll wind up marrying you, Alice Eastman."

She couldn't think of a thing to say, so she simply backed away from the Chevy, feeling her blush deepen. When her eyes met Dylan's again, she couldn't look away.

He couldn't either. Suddenly, he sounded breathless. "It could happen, you know."

"Us fall in love?" She was skeptical. Besides, he was being ridiculous. She was still in junior high. And he'd be going to Rock Canyon High. "I guess time will tell."

His low sexy laugh carried more promise than any sixteen-year-old boy's should. "Time might tell, Alice," he returned. "But I never would."

He'd all but come right out and said they'd have sex someday! Somehow, she managed a droll smile. "We'll see about that, Dylan Nolan," she managed to say. And then she simply turned away, coyly tossing a long braid over her shoulder, the way the older high school girls did.

"We sure will, Alice," he called after her.

With every fiber of her being, Alice wanted to skip, but she forced herself to walk away slowly, gently swaying her hips as if she was already Dylan's woman. She was only thirteen, but she already knew her own heart. She could definitely fall in love with Dylan. So what if he was joking? She *would* marry him. Of course, it would be years from now....

Meantime, she'd forget all the silly speculation about the stalkers, murderers and psychopaths who'd supposedly followed him to Rock Canyon. After all, nobody was going to murder *her!*

It would be years before Alice had good cause to revise that opinion.

"I'D RATHER LOOK at you than talk about all the bad stuff that's happened, Alice." Dylan pulled his new Ford truck near a secluded grassy spot in Cat's Canyon that he and Alice had long ago claimed as their own.

She shot him a coy glance as he turned off the engine. "Well, look."

"How could I do anything but, darlin'? You look great. C'mon." Getting out, Dylan circled the truck, opened the passenger door and grabbed her hand. As they walked into the grass, toward an isolated hillock surrounded by trees, her pink, ankle-length sundress blew in the breeze. At twenty-two, she was all grown-up, which meant for days, Dylan had been worried about picking her up at the airport. Every time she'd come home from college, Alice had gotten even more sophisticated. And every time the changes unsettled Dylan.

Not that he was doing badly for himself. He'd been working for her father for years, full-time since high school, and with Ward Eastman's health now in decline, Dylan was nearly running the Eastman ranch. Still, deep down, he guessed he was scared Alice would move beyond him someday. Elude him.

Wind up not marrying me.

Alice was watching him. "Thinking good thoughts?"

Dylan took in her face—her pale cheeks and green eyes, the white-blond hair that was cut above her shoulders and artfully held back from her face with clips. "I'm remembering the first time I saw you," he said. "Outside the general store when you were

thirteen." *When I said we might get married someday.*

She grinned. "I was so embarrassed about my
braces."

Smiling back, he said, "You were cute as hell."
Watching her now, he remembered other days—her
sitting on corral fences and catching fireflies, and how
she'd shut her eyes and puckered her lips the first time
he'd chastely kissed her. Of course, lately those kisses
had gotten deeper and more demanding, leading to
fondling that left their bodies damp and hot and the
truck windows steamed.

So, why couldn't he ask Alice to marry him? Why
hadn't he already? The questions sent an unwanted
darkness through Dylan's soul, a deep sense of foreboding, of warning. He'd experienced so many bad
dreams. Time after time, he'd awakened on dark,
lonely nights in a cold terrifying sweat, trying to piece
together his nightmares and wondering about the visions that haunted him. Sometimes he could almost
see a house—a big white mansion, he thought—hidden by trees and surrounded by a high stone wall.

But who did the house belong to? Dylan didn't
know anyone who owned a mansion. And he couldn't
remember more about the lake in his dreams, either—
or the swing set, which was near the lake. Sometimes
he'd lie awake for hours, wondering who'd been
swinging. Had it been him? Had a little friend been
with him? If it was a memory, was his dad still alive?

But no...his mother always said Dylan was still a
baby when his father died.

It's nothing, Dylan. They're just dreams.

And yet he'd described the dream-place to his mother once. She'd assured him it wasn't anywhere they'd visited, but he could swear he'd seen recognition in her eyes. And fear. What didn't his mother want him to remember? Why wouldn't she talk about it? And how could he marry Alice when there was something so dark in him that was unresolved?

Dylan's fingers tightened through hers. "Meet any guys at school last term?"

"Nope." Urging Dylan down with her, Alice sat in the grass, then drew up her knees and hugged them. She grinned. "Meet any cute girls here in Rock Canyon, Wyoming?"

That made him laugh. "None I haven't met before."

"Good."

Dylan sent her a long sideways glance. "Is it, Alice?" *Do you want me? Are you ready to settle down?*

She swallowed hard, glancing away. "I—I want to know what's been happening around here, Dylan."

He shrugged, unease coiling in his gut. He felt so torn between the feelings of foreboding and wanting to rekindle the romance they'd shared when she was home during the Christmas holidays. "Nothing. It's just I've had a bad feeling ever…ever since your prom."

Alice shook her head ruefully. "Who would do that? Call and say your mother was dying? I'll bet it was just some jealous guys from school."

"Probably." That's what the cops had said. After all, Dylan had come from nowhere, and in his sophomore year, he'd become a top scholar and athlete at

Rock Canyon High. Now, neither he nor Alice mentioned the similar calls that had made Dylan miss football games—including the one where a recruiter had come, which possibly cost him a scholarship.

Alice sighed. "And now Mom said someone messed with your mother's credit rating."

Dylan nodded. "A couple months ago. The police said it was hackers. Probably not locals. Just some kids fooling around, nothing personal." Dylan shrugged. "With computers, they could have been from anywhere in the world."

Alice looked relieved. "Well, that's good."

Trouble was, Dylan didn't think the police were right. Slowly, over the years, he'd come to feel that so many small things in his own life didn't add up. His mother had been forthcoming last year when he'd asked about their moves during his childhood, but not all the time lines jibed. And Dylan wanted to know more. Especially about those…dreams.

Or memories.

He was probably being paranoid, but he'd started to wonder if the disturbing calls were connected to the dreams. *Or my father.* His mother said Dylan was a few months old when he died, and that talking further about him upset her. Since she'd loved him so much, she said, she hadn't even kept any pictures.

But that didn't ring true. It was so unlike Dylan's mother. They had boxes of snapshots from his childhood, from all over the country where they'd lived. So, why hadn't she kept any of his dad? And why was she so closemouthed? On other issues, she'd tell Dylan whatever he wanted to know. He remembered the town gossip when he and his mother arrived in Rock Canyon, too, but that had died down. Long ago, she and Dylan had become respected members of the community.

But what if people were right? What if his mother *had* been hiding something years ago?

His lips parted. He started to open up, but then decided Alice didn't need to hear all his doubts and worries. Besides, it was probably all in his head. He glanced at Alice. He was so proud of her. She'd graduated summa cum laude and she'd already gotten a job at the hospital down in River Run. Noticing hair had come loose from her clip, Dylan lifted a hand and brushed the silken strands from her forehead. He loved her hair. It was straight, fine and blond, and the softest thing he'd ever touched. He said, "You still remember when we met, huh?"

Swallowing hard, Alice scooted closer, put her arms around him and hugged him tight. "Yes, and I'm home to stay now, Dylan," she urged softly.

"I'm glad," he whispered, lowering his lips to hers. Years of want was in the gentle pressure, and Alice released a soft uninhibited sigh. Seconds later, she settled her palms on his shoulders and pushed him down into the grass. With a sweet smile, she broke their kiss, lifted her dress and playfully straddled him. His breath caught at the feel of how little fabric was between them, especially when she began rocking herself over the quick-hardening swell of him. His hungry eyes watched her unbutton the front of her dress.

"Alice—" Breathlessly, he reached a hand to stop

her. He couldn't believe it. Didn't she know what she was doing? Sure, he'd touched her and kissed her breasts, but only when they were inside his truck, and in the dark. This was broad daylight. Licking his dry lips, he watched her release the front catch of her bra. Then the hand he'd raised to stop her edged aside a bra cup, and his gaze warmed on her breasts, which were small, pale, and perfect, with pert rose-tinged tips.

"Alice," he said again. This time he tried to tease, but his voice came out hoarse. "You trying to seduce me here, darlin'?" Were they about to go all the way for the first time?

She giggled nervously. "Yes," she whispered. "I think I am, Dylan Nolan." Leaning, she pressed her mouth to his again. Coming closer still, she brought her breasts to his chest and rolled her hips, so he could feel her heat through her panties where she'd settled over his straining fly.

Moaning, he gave her more tongue, thrusting it deeper, his mouth soul-kissing and moving deftly on hers. Pushing both hands up, he found her breasts and teased the nipples, then his palm slid down, catching her hip, urging her to move faster on him, showing her how to ride him. They'd never lain like this, not with so much room or with her on top, and every touch was hot magic. Already, her movements were gloriously erratic, her breath excited.

Gasping against her mouth, he raggedly whispered, "Does it feel good, Alice?" He knew it did, but he wanted to hear.

"Yes," she whimpered, languorously moving herself on the hard ridge of him. Her voice got raspier, more urgent, so low he barely heard. ''I want to take off my panties,'' she whispered with no guile, only longing. ''I want us to make love, Dylan.''

Had he really heard right? His heart hammered, his voice felt strangled. ''Alice, don't you want to wait? Don't you want a bed? It's our first time, so—''

''No.''

The nipple he was still rolling between a thumb and finger was hard and aching, and her womanly heat was steadily pressuring where he was getting so painfully ready for her.

''I imagined it right here, Dylan,'' she gasped. ''Just like this. Where we used to hang out when we were kids.'' Running her hands through his hair, she let the straight golden strands fall through her fingers. Emitting another whimper, she stopped moving. A whoosh of breath left him. More than life, he wanted to beg her to start loving him again. He'd love her back, too. He'd deny her nothing. Never. Certainly not the sweet loving tenderness in his heart now. Leaning his head back a fraction, he hoarsely said, ''I've never been with a woman. You know that, right?''

Her eyes widened. ''I thought maybe while I was away at school…''

''Don't you know?'' he continued huskily, his whole body aching for her. ''All these years, I've waited for you. I love you, Alice. I've never wanted— or been with—anybody else.''

Tears shimmered in her eyes that were so like the

color of the grass. "Me, neither. I love you, too. Marry me, Dylan?"

He nodded. "All these years, you knew I would."

"Yeah, I did."

Emotion tore at him as she started to struggle upward. Wherever she was going, he stopped her by brushing his lips across her breasts. Flicking his tongue over the tips, he paused and suckled, the taste alone making him moan. He couldn't get enough.

When she got up on her knees, still straddling and unbearably arousing him, he could merely stare at her—at the hard, dark peaks of breasts he'd kissed and the soft silken slopes of her belly and hips. She'd brought him near the edge, throbbing with want.

"Here," he said. Holding her and rolling over, he gently, wordlessly urged her back, so she was lying on her open dress. Soft, hungry eyes watched him as he kicked off his boots, unzipped his jeans and slid them down his hips. She stripped down her underwear and opened her knees as he kneeled before her. Crouching close, he moved quickly into the cradle of her legs, using a hand to guide his hard hot length to her, and then he cupped her face with a free hand, loving the silken feel of skin against his work-callused palm. His throat felt raw. Even the light summer breeze was strong enough to sweep away his voice—it was that low. "Sure you don't want a college boy, darlin'? You're really ready to settle for this rancher?"

Her eyes were dreamy, making her look far away and yet close. "I want you," she whispered, her voice catching as she arched to bring him inside her body. "I always have."

Feeling her damp slick flesh start to close around him stole his smile. Hers vanished, too, and her eyes suddenly shone again with tears. Staring into them, Dylan could see his own emotions reflected there. "I'd give my life for you, Alice," he whispered.

"But you'll never have to."

"But I would," he whispered back. And then he pushed in, going straight to her core, bringing his heat to hers. At the joining, doubts and fears vanished. Crank callers, lost memories and worries about a father he'd never known were entirely forgotten.

Someday the past might come calling. Maybe Dylan even knew, deep down, that the unspeakable past would bring unparalleled danger.

But not today.

Today there was only Alice, the light in his darkness. And only this idyllic secluded grassy place that belonged to both of them where no harm could ever come.

"ALICE, snap out of it. What are you thinking about, girl?"

Loving Dylan.

Alice Eastman Nolan had been thinking of the day they'd first met outside the general store, and of the day they'd made love in Cat's Canyon. Was that really only a year ago? she wondered mistily. And was it really ten whole years since she'd met Dylan? Now she forced her mind back to the present—and her bridesmaid, Jan. "I was just wondering why I can't hang up this veil. It keeps slipping off the hanger, Jan.''

"Here, let me help.''

"Nope.'' Clad only in white lace panties and a bra, Alice turned away from her wedding dress, which was neatly hanging on the back of a door. Grinning at Jan, Alice held out the floral headpiece from which the veil hung, surveyed it, and then simply walked over and settled it on Jan's head. "Look, why don't you just wear it? Between the veil and the bouquet I'm throwing you, maybe Leland'll get the message today and propose.''

Jan lifted the veil. Sadness touched her eyes, despite her smile. "I hope Leland will. But I always thought…'' Jan's cheeks colored. "C'mon, Al. We both know Leland had a thing for you back in high school. He was so jealous of you and Dylan…''

Leaning, Alice squeezed her best friend's hand. "Maybe. But everybody knew Dylan and I would wind up together. And now we have. As of today, I'm an old married woman. Things have changed. Leland loves you, Jan.''

The words chased the doubts from Jan's eyes. She laughed. "Yeah. I think he does. I guess I'd better go find him. Maybe I can round up Dylan, too, while you finish dressing.'' She blew out an envious sigh as Alice stepped into the skirt of a gray linen suit. "I sure wish I was headed for Hawaii and a honeymoon.''

Alice playfully brought the veil over Jan's face again. "You look like a bride already.'' It had been an all-white wedding, and with the veil down, Jan could have been a stand-in for Alice. "Now go and find Leland," Alice urged with a soft, encouraging laugh. "Ask him what he thinks of the outfit. He'll get the picture."

"I don't know," Jan said with a smile. "Men can be pretty dense." She headed for the door, then turned. "How do I look?"

Alice did a double take. "Exactly like me. We could be twins." Jan's light blond hair was hidden under the veil, and the simple floor-length gown was a near replica of the one Alice had just taken off. "Now go on."

Jan smiled. "I'm going."

Alice waved her through the door. After she'd gone, Alice continued dressing, putting on a blouse and jacket, her mind racing ahead to tonight when she and Dylan would make love—and maybe a baby. Sighing and turning this way and that, she toyed with the scarf she intended to wear. After a few moments, she settled on simply knotting it in front.

"There," she whispered with satisfaction. "That's it."

Suddenly, she cocked her head. Had she just heard something? Turning toward the closed door, she raised her voice and called, "Jan? Jan, is that you?" Was someone in the hallway?

No one answered.

Her eyes narrowing, Alice slipped into her heels and headed toward the door. She opened it and stared out, looking in both directions. A slow, unexpected shiver passed down her spine. The hallway was long and dark, and she'd seen no light switches.

Maybe Dylan had come down here to surprise her. "Dylan?"

Alice took a tentative step into the hallway. She heard nothing, and yet…she had the strangest feeling she wasn't alone. Fighting another shudder, she wished this deserted wing of the church didn't seem quite so creepy.

"Don't be silly," she whispered, knowing she was being ridiculous. She and Dylan had just gotten married here. It was hardly a dangerous place.

But then a scream sounded. Her head jerked toward the high-pitched single note. It was coming from the end farthest from the reception. Alice's heart hammered. Something had happened to Dylan! That was her first illogical thought as she started running. As she neared the place she thought the scream had come from, it was abruptly cut off. As if someone…

Has just been killed!

It wasn't Dylan, though. The scream was a woman's. Alice knew that now. But was it Jan? Had Jan tripped or fallen, maybe? Speeding her steps, Alice thanked God she was a nurse. If Jan was hurt, she'd know what to do. Her heel slid across the slick wood floor. She skidded, then caught her balance. Rounding a corner, she hit the hallway where Dylan was supposed to go to change. Weak light was coming from a half-open door to the choir's robing room.

Alice's palms hit the door. As she rushed inside, her eyes landed where a stained-glass window reflected light on the floor. It looked as if colored pieces of paper had been strewn across the wood. Except one of the red spots wasn't a reflection of the decorative glass. It was a widening pool of liquid.

Blood!

Alice gasped, her eyes fixing on Jan.

Racing forward, tears springing to her eyes, Alice stared at the back of the white dress. It was slashed with blood. Jan's blond hair was barely visible beneath the veil, but it was definitely her. Going to her and rolling Jan over, Alice forced her frantic hands to seek the wound. Or wounds. There were many, Alice realized. *And oh, God, the worst wound's to the heart!* Even as she pressed Jan's chest to staunch the blood, Alice realized Jan was dead. Yes, blood was only eddying in the gashes now because Jan's heart wasn't pumping anymore. Raising a hand, Alice shoved aside the veil and pressed Jan's neck. But the pulse was gone.

"She's dead," Alice whispered. Lord, what was wrong with Alice? Why wasn't she moving more quickly? She was a nurse—and yet everything was different when it was your *friend* who was...

Dead!

Suddenly Alice jerked her head toward the open door, realizing *she* was in danger. A murder had just occurred here! The killer could still be in the room. Her eyes fixed on the door. Was someone behind it? Hiding? It was so dark in here....

Powerless but to stare at the white dress and veil again, and into the staring empty eyes of her best friend, Alice now understood she herself was probably the intended victim.

How do I look? Jan had asked.

Exactly like me.

Wrenching around—Alice's eyes locked with the door just in time to see it slowly shutting. Someone *was* behind it!

Moving too fast, she scurried back and slipped in blood, then had to fight the burning bile rising in her throat. Turning, she quickly swiped her hands down her skirt, smearing off the blood. If her hands weren't dry, she couldn't defend herself. And she couldn't get out of the room now. Backing up, she nearly tripped over Jan's body. Her stomach lurched.

And the door finished swinging shut.

"Thank God," Alice gasped in relief. "Oh, thank God." Behind the door was the four-year-old ring bearer from the wedding party.

"Dylan," he whimpered, his eyes wide with terror, his teeth chattering. "Dylan killed Jan. I saw him kill Jan and then he ran away."

Chapter Two

A year and a half later

"Who is this?" Alice demanded. She hugged her waist, anxiously clutching a handful of the navy dress she'd chosen to wear during her second marriage, this time to Leland Lowell. When there was no response, she curled her hand more tightly around the phone receiver. "Why don't you say something!"

There was still no answer, only harsh, barely audible breathing. It was the seventh such crank call today. Alice snapped, "This is somebody from the *Rock Canyon Reporter,* right?"

It might have been, because the line went dead.

Sighing, Alice slammed the receiver into the cradle. Ever since the recent announcement of hers and Leland's marriage, the paper had rehashed Jan's brutal murder, Dylan's disappearance and the accusations against him—as if Dylan could actually commit a murder! Sudden tears welled in her eyes. Well, she guessed the intrusive interest of local journalists was to be expected, since Jan's murder was one of the few such events in the entire history of Rock Canyon. "Still, I wish they'd stop!" Alice burst out. Why couldn't people just leave them all alone? This was hard enough on everyone. Jan's father, Sheriff Sawyer, had done everything he could to find his daughter's killer. And then, months later, Nancy Nolan's attacker.

Alice shivered, and it had nothing to do with the bleak, dark snowbound landscape beyond the window of her father's study. Her heart suddenly squeezed tight. *Her father.* The cancer that Ward Eastman had fought for so many years had finally claimed him in September.

Now Alice's throat threatened to close, and a soft gasp escaped. Dylan was gone, her father was gone, and she felt so alone. *Oh, God, don't start crying!* If she wasn't careful, she was going to lose it. Again. How could so much pain be visited on one person? she wondered. What had she done to deserve all this? What had Leland done? Or Jan and Dylan?

A year and a half ago, they'd all been so happy. Jan and Leland had been on the brink of an engagement. Alice, herself, had been so sweet, so innocent. The proverbial happy blushing bride.

"And a fool," she muttered.

Why hadn't someone—her mother, maybe—told her how fast one's luck could change? Now Alice found herself recalling happier times and the preparations for her wedding to Dylan: choosing the music, which had been Mozart's *Adagio* from a sonata in E-flat. And the bright spring wildflowers, and the matching, white dresses…

One of which had wound up being covered with blood.

Remembering how Jan had looked, lying in a pool of her own blood, Alice shut her eyes. How could she have been prepared to find her best friend murdered? Or to have her new husband accused by a child eye-witness of the murder?

After Dylan vanished, Alice had simply collapsed. Oh, she knew she should have been comforting Nancy Nolan, but she'd done what her father's doctor told her, taken to her bed. Alice had washed down all the pills they'd prescribed, too—the mood elevators, antidepressants and Valium.

Until the day, last summer, when Nancy Nolan was attacked in her cottage on the ranch property, and so badly beaten that she'd been in a coma ever since. The police said it looked as if she'd stumbled upon a burglar during a standard break and enter. Other people, Sheriff Sawyer among them, were convinced Dylan had come back. Dylan had killed Jan, at least according to the sheriff, and then Dylan had returned to murder his mother. So the logic went.

No one would listen to Alice. Lord knew, she'd begged and cajoled. She knew whoever killed Jan also might have killed Dylan, since Dylan would never leave without explanation. Sure, the sheriff looked for clues. But Alice knew he hadn't looked hard enough.

Instead, there'd been psychological speculation: that the prospect of having a wife had awakened a long-buried hatred of women in Dylan Nolan, which was why he'd snapped on the day of his and Alice's wedding. Because they were dressed exactly alike, obviously, Dylan thought Jan was Alice when he'd plunged the knife into her chest. So the sheriff said. Later, when Nancy Nolan was attacked, he said that made sense, too. Dylan had returned to kill the woman he had feared most as a little boy—his mama. Didn't all male killers hate their mothers? And weren't a lot of serial killers just like Dylan—intelligent, talented golden boys whom you'd least suspect? "Just look at Ted Bundy," the sheriff and townsfolk had said.

But Alice knew better.

She'd loved Dylan Nolan since she was thirteen years old. He could never kill anyone. Definitely not her. Nor would he ever leave her. All those fool lawmen had opened and shut the case too fast. Didn't they understand that they'd never know the real perpetrator? Or his or her motivations?

No, there was only one reason for Dylan's disappearance. He was dead. Otherwise, he would have contacted Alice. Deep in her heart, Alice was a hundred percent convinced that whoever killed Jan had killed Dylan, too. And last year, that same person had tried to murder Nancy Nolan.

Even worse, that vile monster was still free.

Alice shut her eyes, thinking of Nancy, lying in a coma at the River Run Hospital. In a strange way, the attack on her mother-in-law had energized Alice. It had made her want to fight back. The day she'd heard about it was the day she'd risen from her bed and walked.

Dylan had been gone a year when she got up and

resumed the nursing job she'd started before her marriage. Now, it was Alice who patiently exercised Nancy's limp body every day, and who prayed that her ex-mother-in-law would revive from the coma.

Every day, while Alice checked the pupils of Nancy's unseeing eyes, Alice's emotions stirred. No, she'd find herself thinking, whatever bastard killed Dylan and Jan and hurt Nancy was never going to get the best of Alice Eastman. Alice was older now. Wiser. Angrier. She knew life was precious—and she wasn't giving up. Yeah, she dared that SOB to come near her. Without so much as a blink, Alice Eastman would very calmly take down one of her daddy's old shotguns and kill him.

The phone rang again, startling her. Snatching it up, Alice brought it to her ear, but only heard a dial tone. She slammed it down again.

No doubt, it was a nosy reporter from the *Rock Canyon Reporter,* gauging Alice's mood and trying to get a quote. "How do you feel about getting married again today, Alice?" he probably wanted to ask. "Don't you fear a replay of the events of your first wedding?"

No, she wanted to shout. *Because this time there aren't any bridesmaids. Jan's dead, remember? Dylan's gone—probably dead, even if the sheriff never found his body!* Anger laced with foreboding flooded her. Sometimes she wondered about the crank calls Dylan used to get when he was in high school. What if one of the kids they'd grown up with—some boy who'd harbored jealousy over Dylan's accomplishments—had murdered Jan and Dylan? Alice had tried to discuss the matter, but Sheriff Sawyer and the police already had an eyewitness to the murder. They weren't looking for further proof. Or suspects.

Not that Alice blamed the sheriff. The four-year-old ring bearer had said exactly what the sheriff wanted to hear. In light of the testimony, it was easy for Sheriff Sawyer not to ask more questions, to ignore the problems with the child's story—that he was only four, that he was traumatized, that the room was dark. The sheriff had lost his only daughter. Despite his skills as a lawman, he was a father, too. Quickly naming Dylan as Jan's murderer had let the sheriff rest easier at night.

Alice sighed. Turning away from her father's desk, she caught a glimpse of her reflection in the darkened window glass. She might feel like hell. But she sure looked good. Bags under her eyes were carefully covered by makeup concealer, her hair was pulled back by two simple velvet-covered clips. The tasteful navy knit dress she was wearing for the ceremony was flattering.

Once again, her insides turned to jelly. What was she doing? How could she marry someone other than Dylan?

Because he's dead!

Alice could barely remember the days after her wedding, much less the papers her father had brought her to sign that annulled her first marriage. She'd signed them without even understanding what they were. Later, it was Leland who stepped in and filled Dylan's shoes at the ranch while Ward Eastman's health failed. It was Leland whom Alice began talking to in the evenings when she returned home from work at the hospital—sometimes about the ranch, or her father's health.

And then, one day, she and Leland had started sharing their mutual losses. They'd even speculated on the murder. Leland said he agreed with Alice, that Dylan could never commit murder. For himself, Leland only wished he'd been able to propose to Jan. That way, he'd said, Jan would have died knowing how much he loved her. But Leland loved Alice, too. At least he had in high school. Which was why they'd come to an understanding.

Dylan and Jan were never coming back.

And Alice and Leland were all that was left.

"But marriage?" Alice whispered now. Dylan had been her one love. Her *life*. Wasn't marrying Leland a betrayal of his memory? Her heart wrenched inside her chest; she was sure it would break. She could live a thousand years, and nothing would ever ease the pain of missing Dylan. He was her rightful soul mate, her lover, her life partner. He was Alice's husband, no matter what the legal papers said now.

Alice could never love Leland in that way.

Staring unseeing into the reflective glass of the window, she decided it looked like a hologram. In it, she could see the objects of her father's study—the heavy mission oak desk and cracked black leather armchairs, the old humidor and cases for his reading glasses. In these past months since his death, neither Alice nor her mother could bring themselves to change the room.

Suddenly her lips parted in mute protest. For years,

a lucky horseshoe hanging above her father's desk had been turned up like a U. "So our luck never falls out, Alice," he'd always said.

Now Alice saw the nail had loosened, and the horseshoe was turned the other way. How long had it been like that? *This year and a half. That's for sure.*

"Yeah, the luck's sure run out," she murmured.

Past the reflections from her father's study, Alice stared into the dark night. Heavy snow lay along tree branches nearest the window, and dagger-like icicles dangled from the leaf-bare boughs. Her eyes followed the long tree-lined driveway down to the ranch's front gate, then to the dark mountains in the distance. Through the woods, the light in her own living room flickered. This past year she'd been staying in one of the ranch's guest cabins, a three-bedroom log cabin that was similar to Nancy Nolan's.

When her gaze landed on her own reflection, Alice still couldn't believe she was even here, waiting for Leland, the justice of the peace and Sheriff Sawyer. She wished the sheriff wasn't going to be present, but he was an old family friend. While it was difficult for him to see his daughter's boyfriend marry another woman, he'd said he wanted to come. And Alice's mother had invited him.

Alice felt a sudden rush of temper. She'd had countless run-ins with Sheriff Sawyer since Jan's murder—all because he wouldn't take another tack during the investigation, and assume Dylan's innocence, rather than his guilt. That meant Sheriff Sawyer was the last person she wanted witnessing her vows to Leland. For years he'd been a family friend, yes. But times had changed.

Oh, how they've changed!

The phone rang again. "Dammit," she burst out, swiftly grabbing the phone receiver again. "Who *is* this!"

More of that damnable breathing came over the line. She twisted the phone cord angrily in her hand. "What? Are you getting a big kick out of this? What's your problem? I dare you to say something."

The breathing stopped. Alice tilted her head. Was he actually going to talk this time? Was this a reporter or not?

"Alice?"

Everything inside her went totally still. She felt as if her heart had ceased beating. She'd know that voice anywhere. Which was why she could barely find her own. She gasped. "Dylan?"

There was a long pause, then, "Yeah, darlin'."

Alice's heart pumped so fast her ears rang. Feeling faint, she grasped the desk's edge and sank into an armchair, her toe catching the waste can and nearly overturning it. Was this really Dylan? Where was he? All this time, she'd been so sure he was dead. What had happened? Why had he run away after the wedding? *Dear God, thank you. He's not dead.* The words played over and over in her mind. *He's not dead. He's not dead. He's not dead.* Her voice shook. "Where are you? Are you all right?"

Only heavy breathing came over the line.

Maybe she'd heard wrong. Her eyes narrowed, and for an instant she didn't trust her own gut instincts.

Had wishful thinking made her *think* she'd heard Dylan's voice? "Dylan?"

"I killed Jan..."

Alice barely heard what followed. She clutched the phone so tightly her knuckles whitened. Gaping, she forced herself to listen. She simply sat there like a doll, feeling unable to move or speak. *Did Dylan Nolan just say he killed Jan? Is he crazy? Why's he saying this?*

"I liked it." The words were followed by a long pause and more forced breathing, then he rambled, "I cut her with a knife. She started gushing. She bled like a pig. You know how that feels, Alice? Warm, that's how. And good. It felt real good."

There was a catching breath that could have been a laugh; the sound brought bile rising into Alice's throat. She still couldn't speak. Or put down the phone. She'd frozen like ice. This wasn't really Dylan! It sounded like him, but she'd made a mistake. A terrible mistake! Beneath her hand, the phone was turning slick with sweat.

"I pushed the knife in," he continued raspily. "In and out. When it came out, it came easy, all greased up with blood. And you know what else, Alice?"

She waited, told herself not to, but then she couldn't stop herself from saying the word. "What?"

"I thought it was you. I said to myself, 'Dylan, you're gonna cut your pretty little wife. Because she's not so innocent. Yeah, you'll show them all how she really is. Cut her until her white dress stinks with blood.' C'mon, Alice. Come with me now. I want to cut you. So, let's go through the looking glass. But don't break it when you jump through. Because the glass'll cut…cut…cut…''

The phone slid from her hand. Cracking against the desk, it tumbled to the carpeted floor, hitting with a muted thud. Grabbing the waste can, Alice dry-heaved, a hard pounding coming into her head from the effort while, crablike, her fingers moved over the floor. Fumbling, she found the phone again. Just as she brought it to her ear, she heard a click, then the dial tone.

Bringing the phone fully into her lap, she clutched it for long moments. For a second she could have sworn it was Dylan's voice. And she'd felt such relief. Had so many questions…

But he didn't kill Jan!

"It wasn't him. It really wasn't. Couldn't have been," she whispered.

Tears stung her eyes. Her helpless gaze darted to the window. Sheriff Sawyer would be here any minute. She didn't like the sheriff, but maybe she should try to talk to him again. And yet what could she tell him? That a man who sounded like Dylan called and confessed to Jan's murder?

"He sounded like Dylan," Alice whispered aloud again in a reedy voice. "He did. Oh, God, he really did.''

And he *said* he was Dylan.

Oh, Alice! Don't you start believing it, too. Dylan Nolan was never capable of murder! He didn't do it. That wasn't him on the phone. Most probably, he'd really been killed by the same person who killed Jan on the day of the wedding. If he was alive, he would have contacted Alice before now. And he certainly wouldn't have called to say...

I killed Jan and I want to kill you, too.

She couldn't remember the exact words, but she could still feel the terror. The shout that sounded from downstairs made her jump. "Alice?"

It was Leland. Her heart was still racing, her hands still shaking. "Be right there!"

"Who was on the phone, hon?"

"Uh...another hang-up call."

She thought she heard Leland say, "I'm gonna sue that darn paper."

Her hands trembling, Alice put the phone on the desk again. She didn't know how long she simply sat there, but the sudden *ee-aw, ee-aw* of a siren sounded, startling her. Hopping up, she nervously crossed to the window. Sheriff Sawyer's county car was stopped at the ranch gate. She shuddered. Who had called? And with whom could she discuss the call? She didn't want to further build a case against Dylan. And Leland was supportive, but recently he'd made clear that they had to move on with their lives....

Is the caller watching us?

Fear flooded her as his words came back. *She bled like a pig. And you know what, Alice? I thought she was you....* The man on the phone knew where she lived. In addition to knowing the phone number at the main house, he probably knew how to reach her cottage.

And he said he meant to kill me.

Swallowing hard, she watched the sheriff's car leave the ranch gate. Because of the slush and ice, he drove slowly up the long straight driveway. As much as she needed to talk, she couldn't tell him. He wouldn't listen. He'd do what he'd done for the past year and a half—hear only what he wanted to.

"I was wrong about the voice," Alice whispered. "It wasn't Dylan. It just couldn't be." Sure, it had sounded like him. But face it, Alice hadn't always been able to think straight. After Jan's murder and Dylan's disappearance, she'd fallen apart, hadn't she? People worried that she'd never really be herself again. Hadn't she taken to her bed, losing herself in a haze? Staring from the window into the sheriff's high beams, she watched the slow movements of the windshield wipers.

Suddenly she squinted. A figure darted through the snow. He was running beside the trees along the driveway, and without knowing it, he was heading straight toward the sheriff's car!

Somebody outside shouted, and Alice realized a second man was chasing the first, probably one of the cowhands from the bunkhouse. Swiftly, she pushed up the window. A blast of arctic air came in the room, making the tieback curtains billow.

"Stop!" the cowhand shouted again.

Seemingly, the man was fleeing the property. He was wrenched around, staring over his shoulder at his pursuer, not watching where he was going. Alice's mouth opened in mute warning as the man burst through the trees, onto the driveway. The sheriff's headlights blinded him. He threw up an arm, but already the car was too close. Trying to save himself, the man jumped up, lunging onto the hood. Momentum made him roll. His head hit the windshield, which cracked, then shattered. The car swerved; the sheriff braked, throwing the car into a spin on the ice. Now the man's limp body glanced off the hood.

Adrenaline surged through Alice. Turning, she ran. As if propelled by a force outside herself, she was barely aware she was moving. Her breath heaved, and her high heels caught on the carpet as she took the stairs. Only now did she register what the man looked like. He was gloveless and hatless. Long-haired, and wearing worn jeans too light for the biting Wyoming winter. Probably a vagrant trying to find shelter in one of the ranch's outbuildings. It would hardly be the first time some poor soul had come out here, looking for a place to stay. "Leland!" Alice shrieked.

She didn't wait for a response. Grabbing a coat slung over the banister, she pulled it on. Outside, icy air hit her. Her stockings were sheer, and she needed a parka, not this dress coat. Her fancy shoes sank into the chilly slush. Not that she noticed. Alice simply ran, the way she always had when someone was in trouble.

Up ahead, the sheriff was getting out of the car, looking dazed, the wire of a radio stretched from his hand. He was talking into the mouthpiece.

"Is he all right?" Alice shouted.

"Sheriff Sawyer's calling an ambulance!" She was close enough to recognize the cowhand kneeling beside the injured man, who was sprawled on his face in the slush. The cowhand shrugged helplessly. "I caught this guy lurking around the back of the house, Alice. Did you tell Leland?"

"He's coming." Alice fell to her knees beside both men, thankful that the professional in her was taking over; the crisis was putting distance between her and the phone call she'd just received. In the last year, she'd learned to thrive on crises. In fact, the more time she spent in the ER at the River Run Hospital, the better she felt. Emergencies meant Alice didn't have too much time to think.

I killed Jan and I want to kill you, too.

Alice pushed aside the voice that was still playing in her head. "Here," she said, prodding the injured man with her ungloved hands. "Help me. We're going to slowly roll him over. I need to get a look at his head."

The cowhand looked nervous. "Shouldn't we wait?"

"For the ambulance?" Alice shook her head decisively. She could already see where blood was matting into the man's thick, wavy black hair. "No, c'mon. Careful there..." Gently, she urged the man's body over.

Even as she probed the gash on his head, she couldn't help noticing the soft, silken texture of his raven hair. Or that he'd be devastatingly handsome, if he weren't so thin. But the face was gaunt, chiseled by slashes of hard bone. He had high cheekbones, hollow cheeks, but his lips were unusually full. He suddenly groaned, the lush lips parting, exposing teeth oddly perfect for an indigent. His thick jet eyelashes fluttered. And then he opened his eyes.

For the second time that day, everything in Alice stilled.

She'd never seen this man. But she knew the eyes. Or thought she did. Yes...she'd know those liquid brown eyes anywhere. They were eyes that belonged to a man accused of murder. A man she loved. A man whose voice she'd only thought she'd heard tonight. It was this man whose disappearance had filled her heart with so much terror—and whose reappearance now filled her eyes with tears.

"Dylan," she gasped. "My God, it's Dylan."

Chapter Three

Was he in a jail cell? No, a hospital. He was sure of that much because harsh astringents and alcohol filled his senses, and the scent of strong cheap detergent from the sheets. But was he lying on a table? No...a bed. He had to think back, to remember what had happened. How badly was he hurt?

"Get a picture from that side."

Through shut eyes, he felt the white *poof* of a camera's flash, and then aftershocks of pulsing, pounding heat on his brain. What the hell were they photographing here? His mind? Wincing, he tried to open his eyes, but the fluorescent light in the room was worse, blinding. Some time ago, he could have sworn he felt people toying with his hands. Had they been fingerprinting him?

A woman said, "His pulse is—"

He didn't hear the rest. A stabbing pain shot through his head. No matter how hard he tried, he couldn't lift his hand to touch it. The all-consuming, body-numbing pain was too excruciating, like nothing he'd ever felt. In addition to that, the painkiller they'd given him was dragging him down, making it hard to think. Fighting a rush of queasiness, he felt himself going further under—deeper, then deeper. Dammit, he had to stay alert. He had to hear what people were saying.

But no one said anything. A wave of darkness washed over him, making him drift again, float. Damn them for giving him drugs that fogged his mind. *Don't shut your eyes. Don't ever shut your eyes. Keep them open or you'll die.*

Where had he heard those words? Who had spoken them? Thought them? Had it been him? He couldn't remember. In his mind, he felt as if he was screaming, but he knew he wasn't making a sound. For a second, there was only the pain, and then the sinking sensation again. Dark murky water seemed to wash over his open eyes, but they were really shut.

"Hold still," someone said.

Had he moved? He felt sure his arms and legs were restrained. Yes, he thought he could feel straps on his wrists. But maybe that was just an IV. Or...

Wait a minute. Had he been arrested? Had they really just fingerprinted him? And could you arrest an injured man? He wasn't sure.

He'd been running; he remembered that much now. Someone had been chasing him, gaining on him. But he'd kept running, his shoulders aching from the frigid cold, his knees stiff, his lungs hurting from stabs of icy air. He'd wrenched his head around so he could keep tabs on his pursuer. As his pounding feet hit the paved, tree-lined driveway, he'd gasped.

Suddenly, blinding white light had filled his vision. Headlights, he'd realized, just a foot away.

"Leave him alone. I want everybody to leave him alone now. I'll take care of him."

Alice.

She was here! That was her voice. Now more pieces fell into place. *She* was why he'd come here. He'd been outside the ranch house, hidden behind a tree. Staring through the window, he'd been watching her. The cowhand had caught him, and then he'd gotten scared. He'd run...

Now he had to see her, but opening his eyes hurt too much. He moaned. He wanted—no, deserved—to touch her. She was so close now. If she leaned, he could catch her scent.

Such a pretty little wife. I'll cut her sweet flesh into ribbons.

The words played in his mind.

And suddenly, the pain returned—stabbing and stabbing at his head—stealing his consciousness, making everything go black.

"ALICE, you'd better stop right there."

Lengthening her strides, she continued down the long corridor, toward the nurse's station, with Sheriff Sawyer gaining on her.

"Alice, I said stop."

Realizing he wasn't giving up, she forced herself to turn around. Over the sheriff's shoulder, she could see into the injured man's room. He was slowly collecting himself, swinging his long, jeans-clad legs over the side of the bed, holding his head with both hands.

All Alice wanted to do was stare, but she pretended not to pay too much attention to him. "It's late," she said. "And I'm tired." Her head was pounding from emotion and lack of sleep, her mouth tasted like stale coffee, and her dress shoes had started to pinch. For hours, Sheriff Sawyer had been giving her far more flack than she was prepared to take. Now Alice just wanted to put the wounded man into her car and get out of here. He'd been cleaned up, but he was still a mess. He was bruised; his gashed head was bandaged. Shattered glass from the windshield had left a deep cut on his thigh.

She glanced around the hallway. Lights from the fluorescent tubes overhead bounced off the glossy white walls and polished tiles; squinting against them, she stared steadily back at the sheriff. "What exactly do you want from me?"

"You know what I want."

She shrugged. "This is none of your business."

"The hell it isn't." He stopped in front of her, black eyes blazing. He was formidable, a big muscle-bound man with a quick temper. Thrusting a stubby-fingered hand through waves of thick, once-jet hair that was now silver, he continued, "I think you've got some more explaining to do."

"Explaining?" Alice's temper rose a notch. "I'm not a kid anymore, Sheriff Sawyer. And you've got no right to take this tone with me." She struggled to calm her voice. She had to. For Dylan's sake. Her gaze settled over the sheriff's shoulder, where a doctor was reexamining the man's head. "That man's got a concussion," she managed to say. "Otherwise, he's pretty bruised up and in pain. He needs someone to watch him tonight, and to administer medication. The hospital can't keep him anymore. You heard. Ten minutes ago there was a four-car pileup on the interstate, and they need the few beds they've got left." Her eyes narrowed. "Which means you should be headed over to the interstate."

Sheriff Sawyer's jaw set. "I'm not going anywhere."

His careful scrutiny made Alice's insides hitch with anxiety. She leaned back against the wall, adopting a casual stance, but really steadying herself. "Look. There were no insurance cards in his wallet, and the poor guy says he's got no coverage."

"Uh-huh." Sheriff Sawyer looked as if he wanted to call her bluff. "And that's why you're so intent on helping him?"

"I always help people." That much was true. Alice had a natural inclination for service work, which was why she'd gone into nursing. Of course, tonight was something different. She didn't understand how, but the injured man was Dylan Nolan. His face was completely different, he'd lost weight…but the eyes were his.

Sheriff Sawyer nodded. "Uh-huh," he said again. "And so you want to take a stranger home? To your cottage? Not even to the bunkhouse, so the hands can watch him?"

"What's the big deal?" she said, her defensive

tone indicating that it was the sheriff who was being unreasonable.

Sheriff Sawyer's sudden growl of frustration reminded Alice of how much she and Jan had feared this man's wrath when they were kids. "I'm only asking one more time, Alice. What did you mean when you first saw that man?"

"Mean?" she parroted innocently, buying time to think. Not that it would help. She'd known the man from birth. He could be as tenacious as an angry pit bull. True, he was Jan's father—Alice's best friend's father. But when it came to Dylan Nolan, Sheriff Sawyer hadn't been much help. To assuage his own pain, the sheriff had wrongly convinced not only himself but everyone in Rock Canyon that Dylan was a monster.

But it wasn't true.

Alice knew better. Sure, for a second tonight, she'd thought she'd heard Dylan's voice on the phone, confessing to the murder. But she was wrong. It was as simple as that. And now she had to be crafty. Her eyes settled on the injured man again. His face was contorted in pain now, his head tilted while a doctor probed the back of his head.

Her gaze traveled hungrily over his face. Under the hospital's bright lights, his skin was pale, like chiseled ice. Hard bones lay right below the skin. He had a sharp nose. Well-defined, full lips. Pretty lips, Alice decided, for such a gaunt face. His thick raven eyebrows didn't exactly curl, but rose in diagonal lines above the man's shut, black-fringed eyes. No, she'd never seen him.

But those brown eyes were definitely Dylan's. Her heart pounded too fast as she remembered the call she'd received again. But no, it simply couldn't have been his voice.

Somehow, she forced herself to look away.

The sheriff's voice turned low, demanding. "Dammit, Alice, c'mon. What did you mean when you turned that man over in the driveway?"

"Turned him over?" What was she supposed to say? Her eyes darted around.

The sheriff looked livid. "Outside, at your place. When you turned him over in the snow. You said he was Dylan."

She shrugged. "I was upset. Frankly, I don't know why I said that."

"Do you know that man, Alice?"

"No."

"Ever seen him before?"

"No."

"Heard of him?"

"No." She'd seen the one, fake-looking ID in the man's back pocket. It said his name was Gerald Williams. But it was Dylan. The thick wavy golden hair she used to love running her hands through was gone, but...

She jerked her head toward the door to his room again. "Look at him. See? He's got dark hair, Sheriff. Does that look like Dylan?" He had to have had plastic surgery, she thought. There was no other explanation.

"No," the sheriff said. "It doesn't look like him."

"Well, it's not him. And I'm just trying to help.

That poor man's got nowhere to go,'' she persisted reasonably, though everything in the sheriff's eyes said this wasn't reasonable at all. No way would level-headed Alice take a strange man home with her.

''Nobody's reported yet about whether or not he's registered at any of the motels in the area. And I don't think I need to remind you that there's an unsolved murder in this town.''

Her temper spiked. ''Unsolved? Always seemed to me you're pretty sure Dylan committed that murder.'' Her gaze narrowed. ''Even though there wasn't enough physical evidence to take him to court if he came back,'' she reminded.

The fire in the sheriff's dark eyes burned. He shook his head. ''If your father were alive, he'd have your hide.''

''Well, he's dead.''

''God, you've got a mouth on you,'' he muttered, glancing away. Suddenly his eyes caught hers again. ''You used to be a sweet girl, Alice. What happened to you?''

''A lot,'' she retorted. ''That's what's happened to me.'' *A murdered friend. A husband who disappeared.*

''You can't take that man to your place,'' he said again, his voice rising. ''This is absolutely insane, girl. Do you hear me?''

Maybe it was insane. Because nothing was making sense. The injured man had opened his eyes again, and now she could feel him watching her warily. Even from here, those eyes were as warm and intense as they were watchful. No, she'd definitely never seen that face. Nothing about him was familiar—not his dark hair, straight nose, or the ridges and angles of his face.

But the eyes.

She'd know them anywhere. Because they were soft brown eyes, most people wouldn't look twice. But beyond the brown were yellowish lights making them shine like honeyed caramel.

They were Dylan's eyes.

Alice's heart hammered. She fought to appear calm, and to ignore her self-doubt. But maybe Sheriff Sawyer had a point. Maybe she was crazy. Maybe she was losing it again, the way she had right after Jan's murder and Dylan's disappearance.

Today had been stressful. She could admit that much. She'd been moments away from marrying Leland Lowell when the injured man appeared.... Minutes away from a wedding, when that sick phone call came. Suddenly, Alice felt weak and shaky. She tried to assure herself that the caller had been following the articles in the *Rock Canyon Reporter*. He was calling her, trying to get some sick kicks. He definitely wasn't Dylan. She suppressed a shudder. What if she was just as mistaken about this injured man's eyes as she had been about that voice....

"Alice," Sheriff Sawyer repeated. "Please be rational. You can't take a stranger home."

She tried to focus, to keep her wits about her. "I *am* being rational. Even if you thought I'd gone crazy after my wedding."

The sheriff sighed. "You went through a real rough period, Alice," he said carefully. "But you're better now. Still, I can't let you walk out of here with this man. He was trespassing."

"It's my property," she managed to say. "Mine and my mother's. So, I guess he *wasn't* trespassing, not if we don't choose to prosecute."

"I need a reason to hold him."

"Well, I'm not going to give it to you. He had a couple of dollars in his pockets, an identification card. He's not a vagrant."

The sheriff stared at her. "You can't take him to the ranch! Your mother is alone in the main house, you're in your own cabin. We have an unsolved murder. Not to mention the fact that Nancy Nolan was attacked. And my...my..." The sheriff's voice broke. Reaching, he grabbed Alice's upper arm and gave her a good shake. "My daughter's killer hasn't been brought to justice, Alice."

Fury boiled inside her. "You're Jan's father, and I've known you since I was a kid. I loved Jan, too. She was my best friend. But you convicted Dylan without a jury."

He dropped his grasp, and continued staring at her as if he'd never seen her. She felt herself waver. What was she doing? Was she really going to take some strange man to her home?

"Fine." Stepping away, he jerked his head toward the other end of the hallway. "I'll just let Leland put in his two cents."

Alice didn't budge. She simply stood there, watching the sheriff take long strides toward the nurse's station. As much as he didn't want to, he was probably calling his office. He'd have to leave here and head out to the wreck on the interstate.

"Well?" Leland said, stopping in front of her.

The man she was going to marry today looked every bit as mad as the sheriff. While he was rumored to have a hair-trigger temper, Alice had never once seen evidence of it—not before now. Maybe it was his flashing eyes that allowed her to stick to her guns. Maybe if Leland had looked hurt, or had any real desire to understand, she would have changed her mind, and not taken the stranger home.

"Well?" she said.

Leland's jaw set. He was a wiry cowboy, tall and lanky, with light brown hair and a mustache. Usually he wore faded Wranglers and a thermal shirt, but today he had on dress slacks.

For our wedding.

"What's gotten into you?" Suddenly he grabbed her upper arm with such force that it hurt.

"Leland," she protested, barely able to believe the aggression he was exhibiting.

He didn't let go. "Are you crazy? Saying you're leaving here with some stranger?" He leaned closer, and she could feel his breath on her face. "This was our wedding day—"

Her heart pulled with warring emotions, guilt among them. "It's not my fault a man got hit by a car in the driveway," she ventured, knowing how this must look to Leland.

"Maybe." He edged another dangerous inch nearer, anger coming off him in waves. "But now we've seen to the man."

Her heart kept pulling. As mad as Leland was right now, she owed him so much. "Leland," she tried to explain, "I'm sorry, but…I can't explain everything right now." *Can't explain that I'm sure this man is really Dylan Nolan.* "Helping him…is just something I have to do."

She winced as his grip tightened. "You'll do what I tell you."

Her eyes widened. Flinching, she threw off his grasp. "Leland," she found herself saying hotly, the stress of the day crashing down on her, "we're not married yet."

"We're as good as." He grabbed her again. This time his fingers dug harder into her upper arm.

She couldn't believe this was really happening. "Don't get physical with me. You're scaring me."

And it wasn't just the hold he had on her. His blue eyes had turned nearly violet with temper. There was something incredibly cruel now in the grim, pinched set of his lips. This man didn't even look like the Leland Lowell she knew. Or had been about to marry.

As she stared into his angry eyes, stories about Leland's occasional fights came back to her. "Just male-posturing stuff," Jan had said once. "You know. They go out. Have a few beers. And the next thing you know, all those guys are cracking pool cues over each other's heads."

Now Alice wasn't so sure. Until this very moment, Leland had been nothing but the gentleman around her. He opened doors, pulled out chairs, asked her how her day had gone. And now he'd transformed before her eyes. God help her, she couldn't believe she'd been about to marry him.

He's dangerous.

Using his grip on her arm, he jerked her closer. "I waited a long time for you, Alice."

A chill went down her back. "You waited a long time for *Jan.* I..." Where was the reasonable man she'd been about to marry? The man who had said he could never love her the way he'd loved Jan? Or the way she'd loved Dylan. "Our marriage..." Somehow, the sudden obsessive light she saw in Leland's eyes had pushed the air right from her lungs. "Our marriage was a *convenience*, Leland..."

The steel-like grip on her arms now brought tears to her eyes. *"Was?"*

Only then did she understand what she'd said—and that she'd changed her mind. She couldn't have married him. If the justice of the peace had arrived, probably she would have halted the ceremony before it was over.

Swallowing hard, she glanced over Leland's shoulder toward the hospital-room door. The injured man was no longer visible. Maybe the doctor had taken him for more X rays. She hoped not. She'd thought they were finished here. And she needed to get the man alone. To find out what had happened. To make sure he really was Dylan.

He has to be. Those are his eyes.

Leland was still staring at her, looking murderous. She searched for the words. "Leland, we...we made the decision to get married in good faith. It made sense. You're running the ranch now. And we've got so much in common. Besides, the people we loved most are…'' She glanced toward the hospital room again, toward the man she was so sure was Dylan, and she swallowed hard. ''Gone. Jan and Dylan are dead…'' *Or at least we thought so.*

There was something bone-chilling in Leland's voice. ''So, you're going to leave me high and dry?''

''No. But…'' Even now, when his grip on her arm was causing her pain, she couldn't stand to hurt him. And yet she had to. She couldn't marry him. ''Yes. I guess I am.''

''If you think you're gonna take that stranger home, you're thinking wrong,'' he choked out. ''I've lost one woman to murder. And no woman of mine is going off with strangers.''

Mine. She felt a stab of anger. ''I don't belong to anyone.''

''You belong to me, Alice.''

She didn't think it possible, but the grasp around her upper arm tightened. Pain shot up through her shoulder. ''Leland!''

He let go.

Or she thought he had.

But when she whirled back around, she saw the stranger. His wavy dark hair was slicked back, his brown eyes narrowed and contemptuous. But while Leland's cruelty was borne of pettiness, what Alice saw in this man's eyes was borne of necessity. He'd grabbed Leland from behind. His two strong hands were squeezing Leland's arms, holding them like a vise. ''Leave the lady alone,'' he said.

The voice wasn't exactly Dylan's…but it was close

enough, if rougher and deeper. Alice watched as he abruptly released Leland. Leland staggered a few steps forward, then whirled around. Instinctively, Alice backed up, flattening herself to the wall, and she scrutinized the hallway, hoping she could signal someone to send security guards. She waited for Leland to lunge.

Surprisingly, he didn't move.

Neither did the man. Alice's heart thudded in her chest, making her breath shallow. Her eyes sought his. Yes, they looked achingly familiar. She could swear she'd stared into them a thousand times. But was this really Dylan? Was this possible? Plastic surgery was the only thing that would account for these changes, Alice thought again. She glanced between the two men, feeling the full power of their gazes. Their anger was palpable. Maybe even murderous.

And then it was over.

The stranger broke the gaze, then settled those assessing caramel eyes on Alice. "C'mon," he said simply. "Get your coat, Alice. Let's go."

Chapter Four

Alice. There'd been nothing familiar about the way he said her name. She'd strained her ears, hoping to recognize that voice, to feel a connection or hear some remembered loving softness.

Now he said, "C'mon."

Still nothing. The maniac on the phone had sounded so much more like Dylan than this man. At the sudden recollection of the call, the hairs at the back of Alice's neck prickled. Or was her physical response simply from how this man touched her? She suppressed another unexpected shudder at the feel of his strong fingers curling under her elbow, warming her skin through the navy wool of her dress.

As he silently urged her down the hallway, her feet seemed to follow as if by magic, and she felt ungrounded, as if she were floating over the cold floor tiles. She glanced up, into his eyes—and felt even more unsettled. Yes, she'd recognize these eyes anywhere, but…oh, God! Up close, there was truly nothing else familiar about him. The color of his hair had somehow changed from golden to black, from straight to wavy. His nose was thinner and straighter, his jaw stronger, the cheekbones more noticeable, the lips fuller. As a nurse, she'd witnessed the marvels of plastic surgery, but she'd never seen such extreme changes.

At the very least, she expected to see recognition in his expression now—surely Dylan would wink or offer a knowing smile, something to let her know it was him!—but there was no hint in his gaze that he'd even seen her before, much less ever been in love with her.

That lack of recognition made her head churn with wild ideas. What if Dylan had witnessed Jan's murder and suffered a trauma so severe that he'd run away? What if traumatic amnesia had made him repress memories of the murder—and everything else in his previous life? Had Dylan somehow forgotten who he once was and the love they'd shared? If so, maybe he couldn't even remember ever living in Rock Canyon.

But that was far-fetched. Oh, Alice knew such occurrences were possible. In nursing school, she'd learned of similar real-life cases. But they were rare. One in a million. Which meant Dylan probably remembered exactly who he was.

And who I am, too.

She glanced around the crowded hallway, then ventured in a hushed tone, "Dylan?"

The man stared down, squinting against the pain caused by his injuries, or maybe just against the bright lights of the hospital corridor, Alice wasn't sure which. He grunted softly. "Huh? What did you say?"

The sheer blankness in his gaze was jarring, and

her voice came out sounding strangled. "Why aren't you talking to me?"

"What did you want me to say?"

That you're Dylan Nolan. A group of doctors were passing them, so she said, "Uh...nothing."

He glanced away, steadfastly ignoring her. Those same brown eyes that had looked glazed by painkillers moments before were now fixed intently on the red-digital exit sign above the ER doors. Was he pretending to be more seriously injured than he really was? Alice swallowed hard. She needed to talk to him some more, but there were still so many people in the corridor. And Leland...

She glanced over her shoulder, expecting to see Leland following them, but he was gone. As angry as she felt at his manhandling, a wave of heartache came over her. Leland deserved better than this, even if they could never be more than friends. Alice knew that now. When he cooled off, they needed to have a serious talk. She was sure he'd soon realize that breaking off their engagement was for the best. Still, she wished there was a way to explain why she was leaving the hospital tonight with a seeming stranger.

Seeming being the operative word. She stared harder at the strong, silent man beside her. *Dylan must have had surgery,* she decided once more as her eyes hungrily roved over his dark hair and the hard edges of his cheekbones. There was no other logical explanation. If this was really Dylan—and Alice was so positive it was—he'd changed absolutely everything about his appearance and mannerisms.

Except what was unchangeable—his eyes.

"Here," she managed to say, since he was limping, favoring his right leg. "Let me help." Disengaging her elbow from his hand, she risked slipping her arm beneath his navy pea coat and around his waist. When he stiffened, she felt a sudden, unexpected flare of temper. *Why are you flinching? Don't you want me touching you?*

"I can manage by myself." His words were succinct, coming through clenched teeth.

"You're hurt."

"Nothing's broken."

My heart, she thought, looking into his eyes.

"I don't need any help," he said again.

"I'm sure you don't," she retorted, feeling an undeniable rush of anger. Lowering her voice, she continued, "You've apparently been managing by yourself for the past year and a half."

He pretended not to hear. "What?"

"You heard me." As much as she wanted to, she didn't withdraw her hand. God help her, but she wanted to touch him. *Needed* to.

And yet, as her palm nervously settled over the soft cotton of his shirt, she expected to feel something...more familiar—maybe old, well-worn memories of how his waist felt against her palm, of how her side brushed his. But she only experienced an electric leap of her pulse, the flooding of warmth and excitement at touching him. Even worse, his sheer unresponsiveness tweaked something deep within her, challenging her so much that her heart thudded hard against her ribs. And yet, what if she was wrong, and this wasn't really Dylan?

She was about to try asking him again when a co-worker appeared. "Didn't think you were working tonight, Alice," the other nurse said, her eyes curious. "I thought you were…"

Marrying Leland. "I'm not working." Somehow, with her hand still settled on Dylan's waist, Alice managed a smile. "Just down here seeing a friend."

The nurse's eyes held female appreciation. "I can see."

So could Alice. She wished she could do something to calm the wild pulse beat in her throat. This had to be Dylan. He was the only man who could affect her this way; there was something magnetic about him that was drawing her physically closer to his side. But now, as they continued walking, she didn't recognize his slow, almost ambling gait. Hadn't Dylan's walk been more purposeful, the pace faster, the strides more clipped?

She fought against the panic and doubt twisting inside her. Lord, what if she was wrong? What if she was really taking some stranger home? And not just any stranger. But a sexy man whose penetrating, assessing gaze said, despite the circumstances that brought him to the hospital, he was no victim. Feeling another overwhelming rush of anxiety, Alice drew in a sudden sharp breath and inadvertently tightened her hand on his waist.

He edged away.

"You're hurt," she reminded him, her voice tight. Her eyes darted around, but the hallway was still too crowded for them to carry on a real conversation. So many emotions had washed over her since she'd first

seen him—first shock and relief. Then fear: Why had
Dylan run away? Where had he been? For so long,
she'd been so steadfast in her defense of him, but
now—if this was really him—he'd appeared so in-
explicably. And he wasn't talking. Soon she'd be
alone with him, she reminded herself. And then he'd
surely be forthcoming with the whole truth.

She just hoped she wasn't losing her mind. Her
throat closed with foreboding as her eyes continued
scrutinizing the man beside her. Dylan had always
been strong, but this man's body looked leaner and
yet stronger. Muscles bunched under his clothes,
straining his jeans at the thighs, pulling the shoulders
of the pea coat. His smell wasn't as she remembered,
either. But maybe that was only because deeper
scents—the natural oils of his skin—eluded her. He
smelled clean and fresh, though, like snow in the
mountains. Probably he'd been outside the ranch
house for a long time, standing in the cold.

Watching me.

She was sure that's what he'd been doing. He
hadn't come to the ranch looking for work as he'd
claimed. She sent him another sideways glance, but
he didn't seem to notice. Before she could stop herself, his name was wrenched from her lips again, now
spoken with fear and a hint of pleading. "Dylan—"

His head jerked toward her, his eyes focusing so
sharply on her face that her cheeks burned. "Lady,"
he said gruffly. "You saw my ID. My name's Gerald
Williams."

Her heart thudded. Her hand on his waist went
slack. *Dear God, what's happening? Why are his eyes*

so like Dylan's? If it's Dylan, isn't he going to say so? Is he really going to persist in pretending to be someone else?

She just wished Dylan would look at her. Didn't he know how disturbing this was? For a year and a half, she'd thought he was dead. His sudden reappearance, looking like somebody else, was like something out of a movie. Had he fled and gotten plastic surgery so that he could return to Rock Canyon, solve Jan's murder and clear his name?

And love me again.

Oh, God. Please, make that be true. As soon as the quick plea was out, her heart squeezed tight, her insides wrenching with emotion. Because if this really was Dylan, then he'd also left Rock Canyon without a word. He'd let her mourn for a year and a half. She'd been so convinced of his death that she'd almost married another man!

What if he stopped loving me?

Or killed Jan. At the unexpected, traitorous thought, the hairs at the back of Alice's neck prickled, and she suppressed a shudder. After all, as much as she was loath to admit it, there was still an eyewitness who claimed Dylan killed Jan Sawyer. And tonight, on the phone, the caller had said he was Dylan, and that he'd killed Jan.

Not that Alice believed it.

Still, there has to be some way to find out positively if this man's really Dylan. Alice stopped in her tracks, eyeing the exit doors. "Wait," she found herself saying. "I have to check on someone." Gripping his waist hard, Alice hit the elevator button.

Whoever the man was, he wasn't inclined to show much emotion. His voice was low, almost gruff, and yet smooth somehow, with an underlying ripple of seductive silk. "We're not stopping, Alice. You can check your patients later. I need to get out of here."

"*I* needed to know you were alive all last year." Tears suddenly stung her eyes. "So I guess we don't always get what we want."

The man who was so intent on calling himself Gerald Williams squinted, looking into her eyes as if she was crazy. Then he said, "I don't know what you're talking about, lady. I guess I was as alive last year as the next guy."

"Why did you disappear?" she asked.

"Disappear?" His eyes narrowed. "I've never even been here before. So how could I disappear? Like I told the sheriff earlier, I was coming around your ranch, looking for work."

She was stunned. And no, she didn't really believe he'd suffered amnesia and couldn't remember her. "You're really going to deny you're Dylan Nolan?" she challenged. "You're going to deny that you disappeared the night of our wedding, when Jan was murdered? You're going to deny knowing me?"

"Lady," he retorted, his eyes narrowing in a near wince from the pain of his injuries. "Don't get your panties in a knot. Whoever ran out on you, I'm not him." His eyes drifted over her. "And I figure if I ever saw you before, I'd remember."

She couldn't believe it. "You'd *remember?*" As if he didn't know her.

"Sure, I'd remember. You're cute."

This was no time for compliments. "Under the circumstances," she managed to say, "that's an entirely inappropriate comment." As she stared into his eyes, something inside her broke. She lowered her voice another notch. "Sorry, but I'd know your brown eyes anywhere!"

He shrugged. "Lots of people have brown eyes."

Her gaze pleaded with his. "But—"

He gave a slight shake of his head. "I don't know who you think I am. And as grateful as I am for your offer of hospitality since I lost my wallet somewhere in the snow and don't have anyplace to stay tonight, I think I'd best be getting along."

She gaped at him. "You mean just leave me?"

The bemused curve of his lips and wariness of his eyes indicated he thought she was a loose cannon. "Uh…yeah."

"You can't."

He stared at her. "Why are you acting like there's something between us?"

"Because there is."

He stared at her. "Mostly empty space, lady."

She didn't know what to say. Was he going to leave her now—just as he had a year and a half ago? Dammit, she knew it was Dylan! "Why are you even here? What were you doing at the ranch?"

"Like I told the sheriff, I was looking for the bunkhouse. I could use some work, and down in town, they said the Eastman ranch was the most likely bet."

She didn't believe a word of it. She looked him up and down. "You just happened to be looking for ranch work in the dead of a Wyoming winter?"

He didn't miss a beat. "That's right, ma'am. A man's gotta eat year-round, come rain or shine."

Turning abruptly, she stared into the shiny stainless-steel elevator doors, feeling another rush of anxiety as she took in his unfamiliar reflection. "Hurry up," she muttered, jabbing the elevator button again with the point of a fingernail.

"Look—" The man beside her sounded suddenly testy as his eyes darted to the exit doors. "I really do want to get out of here."

"Too bad," she told him, deciding two could play at this game. "I'm nice enough to help you..." She paused for effect. *"Mr. Williams,"* she emphasized before continuing. "But I work here. And I've got to check on one of my patients before you leave. If you're leaving with me, that is."

His short sigh was barely audible. "Fine."

She swallowed hard. Maybe it was wrong not to prepare him, but when the doors swished open, Alice moved toward them. He resisted following. When she glanced up, her eyes meshed with those familiar brown ones. Everything in the caramel irises said he was as intractable as she. "You're coming," she said under her breath, "whether you like it or not."

His gaze was hard, flinty. "Bossy, aren't you?"

"When I want my way." She stepped inside and, with a quick glance over her shoulder, said, "Coming?"

The lips of the man she thought was Dylan compressed grimly. "I'm not sure I've got a choice."

Alice smiled tightly as he got in, then she punched the button for the third floor. She trained her gaze on the lit numbers overhead, but from the corner of her eye she saw Dylan.

He merely stood next to her with that intent expression, his jaw rigid except for the occasional quick quiver in his cheek that made him look like the strong, silent type from the movies. Like Gary Cooper in all those old westerns. Or Gregory Peck.

When they reached the third floor, she got out, feeling rather than seeing Dylan close on her heels. She headed down the long hallway, not stopping until she reached the last door, and a dimly lit private room. The second before she entered it, she settled her gaze on the nearest window. In it, she could see a sharp reflection of the man's features. Again, she felt that jarring sensation as she took in those eyes she'd know anywhere set in such an unfamiliar face. Because she kept her eyes riveted on him as she neared the bed, she saw the exact second that recognition hit. His eyes widened. His tall, almost lanky, but muscular body took one of those ambling strides forward, as if he were drawn magnetically toward the bed where Nancy Nolan lay.

She didn't look good. No matter how much Alice worked with her, Nancy continued to waste away. Oxygen and feed tubes were in place; the woman who'd once turned heads on the main street of Rock Canyon was uncharacteristically thin. Even though Alice had recently washed Nancy's once-thick, luxurious hair, it hung limp and lifeless, and her skin was papery, as pale as the sheets.

A soft gasp came from Dylan's lips, and Alice whirled toward him, her heart breaking, the apology for her cruelty on her lips. "She was attacked some months ago in her house. The police and Sheriff Sawyer said they thought she interrupted a break and enter. But I don't believe it. I think the attack has something to do with Jan's murder. I don't know why I think that, but I do—" Her voice broke. "I should have warned you she'd been hurt," Alice continued after a moment, her voice catching with emotion as she moved toward him. "But I had to see your reaction. To know it was you. And now I know—"

His eyes suddenly narrowed, daring her to take another step toward him, and she stopped in her tracks. Whatever emotion she'd seen in this man's face had been replaced by mere watchfulness. Quickly glancing toward the bed as if he'd never seen Nancy Nolan in his life, he then settled his unnervingly intent gaze on Alice. "Do you have other patients to check on?"

How could he react so fleetingly at seeing his mother in a coma? Alice felt stunned. "You're going to deny you recognize her?"

He glanced at Nancy Nolan. "Who is she?"

"Your mother."

He merely raised an eyebrow. "You sure are a pistol," he offered. "Now, c'mon. Do you have any other patients?"

She could only stare at him. "No."

"Good. Let's go."

"All right," she said after a moment. And maybe it was. Getting him to talk might prove futile, but Alice's litmus test hadn't really failed. She'd seen enough of a reaction to know this was definitely Dylan. Recognition had come into his eyes when he'd seen his mom. And shock. Obviously he had no idea Nancy had been attacked.

Which was further proof that he wasn't the perpetrator, as the sheriff had claimed.

Chapter Five

"I wish he'd stop," Alice muttered. All the way back
to the ranch, Leland's truck had been tailgating her
Toyota. She could swear he was aiming to run her
and Dylan off the road. When blowing her horn and
waving at him hadn't made him slow down, Alice
tried driving faster, but the mountainous roads were
dangerously icy. When they'd reached Cat's Canyon,
where she'd first made love to Dylan, Leland had
backed off a little, but now he'd gotten too close
again. Even worse, Dylan had remained stoically silent and was staring out the window, which wasn't
helping Alice's mood. "That's it," she suddenly announced, pulling over.

Dylan—and she knew it *was* Dylan—glanced over.
"Want me to talk to him?"

She shook her head. "No. Please, I want you to
stay right here. If I need help, I'll wave, but I've got
some things to say to Leland...privately." With that,
Alice got out of the car and slammed her door.

Running back to where Leland was now idling in
the road, she nearly slipped on the ice. "Why are you

tailgating me like that?'' she fumed, coming to a standstill near his rolled-down window. "Are you trying to get us all killed?'' She whipped her chin toward a steep dropoff.

Leland stared down from the darkened cab. "I'm gonna be watching you, Alice," he warned simply, the voice carrying an unmistakable threat.

"Suddenly," she returned, her breath fogging the air, "I feel like I don't even know you, Leland. You never acted this way with me before."

"You never walked out on me before."

"Le-Leland." She stammered from the cold or confusion, she didn't know which. "I'm not walking out on you. I'm just—"

"Taking a stranger to your house."

"Yes, but..." *He's not really a stranger. He's Dylan.*

"By this time tonight," Leland continued, his voice little more than a growl, "you were supposed to be my wife. Right now we should be in bed together. It's our honeymoon night."

The venomous cold she saw in his eyes made her blood curdle. "Leland," she managed. "You never loved me. We were only getting married because—"

"I always loved you, Alice."

Something akin to, but not quite panic made her insides shake like jelly. "You loved Jan," she said, feeling uncertain. Alice glanced around, her eyes darting back to the car where Dylan sat. When she turned back to Leland's truck, strong wind hit her face, making her hair blow wildly beneath her hat, her cheeks sting and her eyes tear. Leland leaned closer to the truck's steering wheel, the wide brim of a Stetson shadowing his face. She could barely see him, just a sliver of his clean-shaven cheek, a hint of mustache and his hunched shoulder where the suede of his fleece-lined coat bunched up, hiding his chin.

But she saw his eyes—in her mind. She saw now the darkness in the depths of those eyes that suddenly chilled her to the bone. How had she assumed that the anger people said he possessed would never be directed at her?

"I never loved Jan," he announced fiercely.

At the words, her heart went wild, stuttering with confusion and fear. "You *did...*you did love Jan," she countered.

Leland's voice dropped so low it should have been whisked away by the wind, but it reached her ears anyway, sounding menacing. "It was you I wanted, Alice."

Enough to kill?

The thought came from nowhere. She glanced nervously toward the Toyota, and was relieved to see Dylan had turned around in the seat to watch her. Instinctively she knew he'd protect her as he had at the hospital.

"All this time, Leland," she began again, her teeth chattering. "You told me..." *You loved Jan more than life. The way I love Dylan. You said you and I were brought together through grief after Jan's murder.* "You said you loved Jan. Were you lying about that?" She couldn't even believe the words came from her lips.

"I was with Jan because I could never have you,"

Leland said angrily, his breath coming in fogged tufts. "I wanted to be with you for years, since back in high school, but I didn't have a chance with Dylan in the picture."

The words chilled her. What was Leland saying? That he'd wanted Dylan out of the picture? Had he wanted Jan out of the picture, too? Alice tried not to remember her friend—how she'd looked, lying motionless on her back with blood coming from her chest, soaking the white bridesmaid's dress.

For a second, Alice stared unseeingly at Leland, feeling frozen—no longer from the cold, but from recollections of the horrible voice that had sounded so much like Dylan's. *You know how it felt to kill Jan? Good, that's how. I pushed the knife in and out. In and out. She gushed like a pig. C'mon, Alice, want to come through the looking glass?*

Were those the exact words? She couldn't remember now. All that mattered was that Leland might have been the caller. Had he been trying to imitate Dylan's voice? Suddenly, Alice wanted to run for the Toyota.

"Leland..." She could only repeat her earlier words. "You *loved* Jan."

"I always had feelings for you." The words were gravelly and harsh with Leland's barely suppressed fury. "And tonight we're supposed to be together. We were almost together."

She stepped back cautiously from the truck. It was suddenly clear that Leland had been obsessed with her for years. Her heart was pounding so hard that warmth flooded her, making her insides churn with heat while the freezing wind continued to beat against the exposed skin of her cheeks.

How had her world gone so out of whack? Nothing was as it seemed. Nothing was making sense. Had Leland killed Jan to get rid of Dylan? Even in high school, Leland had treated Dylan as a rival. So, maybe Leland had made those crank calls to Dylan years ago. Maybe Leland had called, saying Nancy Nolan was in the hospital so Alice and Dylan would miss the senior prom....

And now Nancy really is in the hospital, Alice thought, recalling Nancy's once-beautiful body, now limp and wasting away. Lord, had Leland tampered with Nancy's credit rating a few years back? Leland did understand computers; he'd just installed a complicated new system at the ranch....

If he was guilty, how could Alice prove it? Sheriff Sawyer wouldn't believe her theories. That much was certain. "Please," she said now. "Back off. Quit tailgating me. Just go home, Leland."

"I'll go when I feel like it. Meantime, I'll be watching your every move. Be sure of that."

And she was. Leland had almost been her husband, and now he wasn't letting go of her. Terrified, she turned and headed back to the car. When she got in, Dylan said, "You okay?"

She nodded. "Yeah."

But deep down, she knew nothing could be further from the truth.

"OH, ALICE, Sheriff Sawyer told me what you're doing—" Her mother's pragmatic voice came over the line from the main house. "And I know how strongly you feel about helping people in trouble, but you can't let that man stay here."

"Mother, I appreciate your input…but I have to get off the phone," Alice said once more. Turning in the small living room of her cottage, anger fueled her blood when she looked at Dylan. Hours had passed and he was still persisting in not talking to her, in playing the strong, silent type. "Please don't worry," Alice continued. "I'm fine, Mom."

"Are you sure?"

"Positive." Even if she was pretty sure Leland was still out there, parked under the trees in the snow. Right about now, Alice was more worried about him than Dylan. More worried, too, about the phone calls she'd received during the day. The words came back to her again. *Jan bled like a pig. You know how that feels Alice? Good, that's how…* Pinpricks rose between her shoulder blades. What if the caller was out there, watching her as Leland probably was? What if the caller *was* Leland? Her eyes shot to Dylan. That *he* was the caller was something she wouldn't—couldn't—even contemplate.

"What?" Alice suddenly said.

"I said I wish your father was alive," her mother said. "He'd put his foot down."

But her mother wouldn't, Alice knew. Ward Eastman had always worn the pants around the Eastman ranch, while Beryl Eastman had played the perfect, submissive wife. Where Alice had gotten her backbone, she'd never know. Probably from her father.

Either that, or from the cold hard experiences of the last year and a half.

She softened her voice. "Mother, really. I'm fine." She glanced at Dylan again, wondering if she really was. The man didn't even bother to glance at her now. He was seated on her denim couch, watching television and acting just as distant as he had in the car.

His attitude would drive a saint to distraction. In spite of his injuries, and his obvious need to get off his feet, he managed to look thoroughly self-contained. He was acting so aloof. Distant. Unreachable. Take your pick of terms. It was as if he were inside an invisible capsule. He had to be in severe pain, but he hadn't once mentioned the bandaged gash on his forehead or his cut leg. Pain didn't seem to affect him any more than her repeated questions.

"Fine," her mother was saying now. "I can tell you're going to do whatever you please."

Alice's hand tightened on the handset. She loved her mother with all her heart, but there was no way to explain to anyone what was happening to her right now. "Mother," Alice ventured, "I know this seems strange—"

"It's *very* strange. This just isn't like you, Alice. What's happening to you? You used to be such a good girl..."

There it was again. The second time today. "I'm not being bad," she defended. "But a lot's happened in the past couple years and—"

"I don't care what's happened. You can't bring a stranger into your home. I'm worried—"

"I know it's out of character," Alice interjected, "but…"

Her mother said, "I'm waiting."

But this is Dylan. I know it. I saw the way he looked at his mother in the hospital, and now I know I'm not wrong. "Do you trust me, Mom?"

There was a long pause. Then her mother's tired voice came over the line. "Yes. I do, honey. But still—" Then her mother sighed. "Okay, honey."

Somehow, her mother's resigned trust both touched her and made her temper flare. Damn Dylan for walking back into her life this bizarre way, and not bothering to tell her what was going on. Yes, her heart had flooded with relief and love. But that was hours ago. Now she needed answers. Hanging up the phone, she turned to him. "Are you going to start talking or not?"

"About what?" he said lightly.

"Something other than the weather."

He glanced toward the window where the snow was blowing down in sheets. "The weather wouldn't make for much conversation, anyway. It's pretty bad."

"What's bad is how you're acting. How long are you going to keep playing the strong, silent type, Dylan?"

His voice was level. "Quit calling me that. I don't know what you mean."

She stared at him a long moment, then shrugged. "Make yourself at home," she snapped. "But I guess that should be easy," she added, "since you travel so light."

"Light?"

Her eyes drifted over him. "Yes. Surely you've got some luggage stashed somewhere in town?"

His tone was gruff. "Look. You're angry. And I'm causing trouble with your family. If you want me to go…"

"You're not going anywhere," she assured. As her eyes continued falling over him, taking in his body's ropy strength, she felt a rush of purely female awareness. Heartache quickly followed.

A lump formed in her throat, and she looked away from him to stare out at the snow. Had there ever really been wonderful summers? Lazy days of lounging in the long grass, held in his arms? Right now, in the bleak darkness, it didn't seem possible that they'd once made love in Cat's Canyon, feeling warm sun on their bare skin.

Leaning, she flicked on a second lamp that didn't do much to illuminate the room. Usually, she thought of the living room in the cottage as cozy, now it simply seemed dark, wintery. Heading for the wood-burning stove in a bricked-in corner, she opened the doors and gazed at the glowing embers.

"Here." The voice was low and rough as he rose from the couch. "Let me."

She stepped back, watching him take kindling from the woodpile, then add a log. He knew his way around a wood burner, and he worked slowly, building a new fire that would last. His careful, almost calculated movements were somehow so withholding that they made a whole new rush of anger come over her. Since seeing the recognition in his eyes in his mother's hospital room—and then realizing he was going to continue maintaining he was a stranger—she'd been livid. Livid in a way she couldn't hold back, a way she hadn't felt for years, maybe never. Now the anger raced through her body, rushing right beneath her skin, ready to surface.

When he stepped back, she lithely leaned past him and slammed closed the iron doors of the wood burner. They crashed together, sounding like cymbals, and the quiet left in their wake seemed deafening. Drawing a deep breath, she tried to calm herself, but she was too angry—and too conscious of him. She could feel his heat as he moved behind her. He came to a standstill in the center of a braided rug.

Turning, she crossed the living room, headed for a wall unit facing the couch and flicked on the TV. He was scrutinizing the room, taking in the two oak end tables banking the couch, and a blanket of Native American design that her father had bought in Cheyenne. His eyes lingered near the door, on a saddle and a pair of western-style boots she often wore.

"We were at the hospital longer than I thought," she ventured coolly, hoping a new topic might bring some response.

Dylan merely nodded. He hadn't moved, but was still scrutinizing everything. Catching his eyes, she said, "Does the place meet with your approval?"

"Yeah. It's nice." The words were amiable, but his gaze had turned steely.

She arched an eyebrow. "My tone starting to get on your nerves?"

"Maybe."

"Good. I intend it to." Maybe if she got a rise out of him, he'd start being honest.

"Really," he said. "I think I should just go."

She gazed through one of the two living-room windows. Outside, the snow was coming down hard again, blowing in sheets. The Eastman ranch was a working cattle ranch, but cottages such as Alice's dotted the property, some of which were available to guests during the summer months. Although Alice's cottage was separated from the main house by trees, she could see one light, winking between bare, snow-laden branches. It was the light in her mother's bedroom.

Her gaze returned to Dylan. "It's a little cold for having nowhere to go." She crossed her arms. "Why don't you just sit down?"

He offered a slight lift of his shoulder that might have been a shrug, glanced behind him, then sat on the couch again. "I don't want to put you out. Tomorrow, as soon as the sun's up, I'll head out."

"We'll see about that." No matter how intent he was on denying it, she knew damn well he was Dylan Nolan, and he was going nowhere—not until she had some answers.

She expected a snappy retort, but realized his attention had shifted to the TV. And not momentarily. His eyes were glued to the set, his attention so absorbed, Alice could have ceased to exist. She turned and stared at the screen. The national news was on, though Alice didn't recognize the female announcer.

"...was found brutally murdered at his Bel-Air estate yesterday," the woman was saying. The image shifted from her to the open wrought-iron gates of a mansion. ''The murder has rocked Los Angeles. Outside the stone wall of this exclusive, private estate, Lang Devlyn's mourners have been gathering all day. Not since the murder of Gianni Versace by Andrew Cununan have such crowds gathered to witness a crime scene—this time, leaving flowers in memory of the rock icon.''

The sound shifted to a medley of pop songs, while the image shifted to a montage of the once-young Lang Devlyn, signing autographs, zooming down a country road on his motorcycle, singing to screaming female fans while sinuously moving his body, rolling his leather-clad hips.

''While Generation X may not have heard of this song legend,'' the newscaster continued, ''Lang Devlyn fueled the fantasies of female fans in the 1950's with pop songs such as 'Love Me Again' and 'Tomorrow's Dreams' before going on to become one of Hollywood's successful stars. Working behind the scenes, Devlyn arranged scores for films in the sixties, before going on to a decade of producing recording artists of the early seventies, among them Janet and the Sandman, the Tambourine Folk Blues Men, and the Micro-Velvets.

''Today,'' the newscaster continued as the image shifted back to the crime scene, ''the singer who *Life* magazine once called the Man with the Velvet Voice is dead. Tragically murdered in his home, in this isolated, private section of Bel-Air that has also been home to singer George Harrison, actress Jamie Lee

Curtis, Barbra Streisand and former President Ronald Reagan.''

As she talked of Devlyn's fall from grace in Hollywood—to rumors of his increasing withdrawal from society, drug addiction and failed financial ventures—the camera roamed over an estate that was nothing less than beautiful. Surrounded by a high wall and foliage that kept it hidden from the eyes of curiosity seekers and the tour buses that regularly cruised the Hollywood Hills, the inside was a paradise.

Contrasted to the harsh, dark snowy Wyoming winter landscape and the steep Rocky Mountains in the distance, the L.A. estate was bathed in sunlight. Behind the imposing house was a crystal-blue swimming pool in a natural setting with leafy tropical plants and a waterfall. Lush green grounds sloped to a private lake, surrounded by trees and white-flowering bushes. A swing set faced the still water.

The camera paused on the scene, and Alice felt a shudder travel up her backbone, one that started low, right at the base of her spine. It might be sunny and warm in L.A., but the picture was strangely static. There was something creepy about the stillness of it all. The camera lingered on the lifeless image, while the newscaster solemnly detailed what was known about the murder.

Lang Devlyn had fought an attacker who'd beaten and then stabbed him repeatedly; his murderer had viciously, slowly and without passion committed the act while the aging rock icon, now in his sixties, had slowly crawled from room to room of the massive house, trailing blood.

Alice shuddered again, her gaze shifting to Dylan. He was still utterly riveted. His eyes were intent on the screen, his lips parted. And she could swear she saw something more there than horror. It was as if he...recognized the place.

"And so it ends," the newscaster finished. "A distinguished musical career, spanning a half century. A man who fueled the fantasies of so many millions, has died alone. Tragically, with no known survivors..."

Alice suddenly blinked. "You're bleeding," she said, staring at Dylan. "That bandage needs to be changed." Turning away, she headed toward the kitchen, then returned with a damp cloth and first-aid kit. He was still watching the TV.

"Here," she said.

Stopping next to the couch, she deftly removed the bandage, then dabbed his head with the cloth. Jerking back, he grabbed her hand. The movement was unexpectedly quick, the touch electric. She sucked in a quick breath. "I have to," she said, her voice sounding strangled to her own ears. "You're bleeding again."

"I'm fine." His eyes darted toward the door, as if he wanted to go, as if he felt suddenly trapped.

Had the touch of her fingers on his skin bothered him that much? Maybe, she decided. Touching him had made her own heart beat too quickly. So why was the damnable man still denying who he was? Why was he denying what he felt for her?

Her temper flared. He was still holding her hand, so she twisted her wrist and caught his fingers, twining them through hers. "Dylan," she implored, her voice strangled.

As if to fend off her pleas, he rose swiftly to his feet, his body grazing hers. He stared down at her, and the breath left her. Their thighs were touching, their chests inches apart.

She glared into his eyes. "By damn," she said through clenched teeth. "You're going to start talking."

His lips compressed into a grim line, and he gave a barely perceptible shake of his head—just enough of a movement that she registered it, just enough that a lock of his dark wavy hair fell across his forehead, across the gash and into his eyes.

Such beautiful eyes. Her heart twisted with the thought. She remembered the light in them when they'd made love in Cat's Canyon, that first time. He'd followed every nuance of her movement when she'd undressed—her hands trembling on buttons, pulling down the straps of her bra. He'd registered the sudden heat rising in her cheeks when her breasts were free. There was no forgetting that moment. How could he deny it? How could he pretend they hadn't shared that day? That he hadn't taken her fully, in the deepest way a man and woman could share.

In a way that might make him talk.

The thought came from nowhere. And she was conscious once more of his proximity, of his near breath and the heat of his body. He shifted, as if to step away, but the movement only brought his thigh harder against hers. An undeniable tide of emotion grabbed her then, bringing her to her toes, and the force of feeling pushed her into his arms. Desire was maybe even the least of the emotions. Because there was still fear. And so many questions, so much worry.

And love.

She felt that, too. A love that transcended everything else, making her not even care where he'd been. Her palm slid swiftly around the back of his neck, the smooth skin there making her flesh tingle. Tugging, she pulled his head toward her, bringing his mouth close. Then closer. So close he couldn't resist. Forcefully, her lips collided with his and at the touch, she could no longer stop what was about to happen. His body's tension was nothing more than hard-won self-containment. Every flex of muscle against her said it was about to be unleashed.

No, his injuries weren't on his mind now. He couldn't stop wanting her. He loosed a soft moan that curled warmth right into her bloodstream. As her tongue greedily thrust against his, heat fanned out, then flowed inside her. A needy sound came from somewhere deep, from his heart or soul maybe. "Alice," he gasped against her lips.

It sounded like a protest, but she didn't care. Already, her hands were gliding under his shirt, over ridges of ribs and the hair of his chest, exploring the man she was so sure she remembered. A man who simply had to be her husband, Dylan Nolan.

Chapter Six

He urged her from the windows toward the hallway, as the first kiss punctured a plastic bubble he'd been hiding inside. The second made his heart wrench. The third flooded him with memories. He'd been fooling himself, thinking he could come to town without seeing her. All this time, he'd planned to come back, but never to her arms. He'd meant to ignore her, at least until he cleared his name and found whoever had threatened to kill her. And other concerns plagued him, too. All his own terrifying, haunting memories...

Until he'd actually seen her.

And she'd offered to let him stay with her...

He'd felt completely powerless to say no.

Now, with her body pressed to his, nothing about the past seemed to matter. He couldn't resist her, no matter how many reasons he should ignore the urgent need overwhelming him. When her lips molded over his again, their fit was so perfect and hot that all the pain wracking his body fled.

How could he have denied this feeling? Impossible, when kissing her did such funny things to his blood.

It was racing, but slowing, too; thudding at his neck and flooding his loins while her scent made him pull her nearer. He wanted to share everything.

"Alice," he managed to say hoarsely. *I've missed you.*

Her tongue's caresses moistened his parted lips, then thrust deep inside his mouth. As her fingertips sought and rubbed at his shirt, she offered even more, pushing her tongue deeper, dipping and probing. The emotion of the kiss—and the lust he felt—tore a sound of need from him.

But he had to stop. Because—God forbid, he thought with sudden panic—he could accidentally take her somewhere dangerous. Despite the warnings of his own mind, his arms swept around her, both palms pressing down her arching spine, forcing her to stretch against him. She felt warm and feline. So damn, groin-achingly sinuous. Moaning softly, she opened her legs for him.

His palms moved hungrily then, roving unrestrained down the rest of her back to her bottom. Pressuring her backside, he brought her to his able heat. Just like his hands, his strong, hot, knowledgeable tongue moved in circles, cunningly swirling around hers as he backed her to the wall. Her shoulder blades hit it first, then her back. She gasped as he snatched up the hem of her dress. Slipping a hand between her legs, he sighed with pleasure.

All night, he'd been aware of her legs—of the curves, of the luminous rose skin gleaming through the sheer stockings. Now a stockinged foot slipped from a high heel, and she used a foot to stroke him, her instep curling around his jeans-clad calf as she writhed against his hand.

Heat shot into his groin. The scent of her natural musk overwhelmed him. Moisture soaked her panty hose, then his hand, making his heart beat erratically. Dammit, he swore silently. Alice had recognized him. He should have known she would. There was no way she could mistake him for someone else. Not after the things they'd shared. It was why she was giving herself so easily....

And why he wanted, with a quiet, heartfelt desperation, to oblige. His mind was still reeling from the night's events. Earlier, when his head cracked against the sheriff's windshield, he could have sworn he was going to die. Pain had exploded in his skull, bringing a flash of scary white light, the kind that said he was done for.

But then he'd seen Alice again. He'd blinked, and she'd simply seemed to appear from nowhere, as if from a wonderful dream. For a second, he'd forgotten he was hurt. He'd been transfixed, staring at the stray strands of her light blond hair waving in the wind, seeing her uncertain eyes brimming with tears.

"Dylan," she'd said, her voice catching. "It's Dylan."

Somehow he'd refrained from touching her. He'd longed to stroke her wind-cold cheek and fasten his lips on hers, and wrap his arms around her and hold her as he was now. But he'd stopped himself. Looking into her cloudy, confused eyes had sobered him, bringing him back to earth and making him cognizant of their situation. Hell, he would have run then—he should have rolled away from her, gotten up from the wet, snowy driveway and brushed the shattered glass from his head. He should have clutched his bloody jeans, staunched the wound on his leg and fled as if the devil was on his heels. But he'd been in so much pain; he was bleeding. He'd barely heard the sheriff calling for help because his consciousness was fading. He'd had no choice but to let himself be carted away in the ambulance.

And then he'd seen his mother at the hospital. Damn Alice for giving him such a shock, not that he blamed her. *Oh, God don't think about that,* he decided now, his mouth still moving on Alice's, his heart stuttering. And don't think about the Lang Devlyn estate. Earlier, images of the fancy mansion had kept him riveted to the television screen...

Coming to his senses, he tried to break his and Alice's kiss. He couldn't do this. He had to get busy, and find out what happened to his mother and who killed Jan Sawyer. But Alice clung to him all the more.

And he let her. His own fear and pain only served to heighten his need. He wanted the warmth and assurance of her body; he wanted to cherish the lust coursing through him. He felt alive again. Loved. The loneliness he'd battled for so long was gone. His tongue circled her lips and plunged again.

Gliding his palm up the front panel of her stockings, he pulled the fabric down—her panties, too—

and then pushed his finger deep inside her. Her hips slammed forward and he bit back a cry when her hand slid down from his belt and closed tight over his erection, her fingers molding to him.

He broke the kiss. Wrenching his head around, he thought of going to a bedroom. And then unbelievable need called his lips back to hers. Her mouth was delicate, smaller than his, and as his tongue met hers again, emotion and desire melted into each other. He pulled her panty hose farther down, to her knees, as she undid his belt. As she kicked a leg of the hose away, he ripped down his jeans zipper. The second his shorts were pushed down, their bodies crashed together. He was hard and hot, rising between her legs. Nudging her, the smooth head of him pressed the damp opening.

No protection.

Damn. This moment wasn't exactly something he'd prepared for. No, he was supposed to stay away from Alice. Not that he could. Now he swore to himself that he'd pull out before he came. But he knew he never could. He wanted to come deep inside her—to fill her. How could he want anything other than that? He loved her.

"Dylan," she gasped.

She was ready, so he didn't bother with talk, just entered her fast. Her legs rode up, wrapping his waist. Inside, she was sweet and moist, thirsty. With every thrust, he begged her to drink even more. One of her feet—the one that was bare—slid across his backside, eliciting a shared shudder. Everything felt so damn good it hurt—her toes curling against the back of a thigh, how she bucked against him with both of them so ready to explode. Just the dig of her heel into his thigh made him so weak he thought he'd die from it. His mind raced. *What are you doing? If you don't stop this, we both might die. Someone had threatened to kill her, for God's sake!*

But Alice didn't care about anything right now except loving him. And he didn't care, either. Life without her wasn't even worth living. Shutting his eyes, he buried his face in her neck. He was registering the dampness there, the soft-smelling perspiration, when he felt the sudden clutch of her thighs.

"Darlin'," he whispered, just the way he used to.

And then she let go, the surrender shaking her, and he was taking his own, pushing inside her. Once more. Then twice. And again.

But it wasn't enough—he'd never get enough of her! "Please," he whispered raggedly, his voice raw. *Come.* Pushing hard, he felt her rise to him, and then he flooded her with a release so complete, he knew this would make them a baby.

Our baby!

He'd dreamed about a family. Their family. Little boys who'd catch snails, and little girls who'd look just like Alice. He'd dreamed of how his and Alice's story would end. With the kids asleep. With him and Alice safe and sound, living in one of these guest cabins while he worked the ranch.

But those are just dreams, Dylan. Visions you've

used night after night, to keep yourself going. To pre-tend you can have a future with her.

This was reality.

And reality held the bad things. Danger and death. The murder of Jan Sawyer. The attack on Dylan a year and a half ago, in the church. The attack on his mother. And the cold hard fact that Alice had been about to marry Leland.

As Dylan finished melting inside Alice, he knew he never should have come here tonight. How could he have forgotten that acting like this could get Alice killed?

Even now, he could remember how his lungs had burned, and his terror when the attacker had pulled the suffocating plastic over his head. Even now, he could remember how the tip of the knife blade felt as it teased his neck, how the unseen hand had snatched off the medallion he'd worn.

I'm gonna cut your sweet little wife. She'll think it's you who's killing her, Dylan Nolan. I'll make sure of that. Damn sure.

Instinctively, his arms tightened around Alice as her legs uncurled from his thighs and slid slowly down. As she found her footing, he felt torn. He wanted to tell her everything, starting with how he'd fled the church in terror a year and a half ago. How, since then, he'd done everything he could to disguise himself, including getting plastic surgery, so he could return to Rock Canyon unnoticed and clear his name. He had to do so without Jan Sawyer's killer recognizing him, too—or the man who'd attacked his mother.

He squeezed Alice even tighter. Dammit, she and his mother were everything in the world to him. *And someone wants to kill them.*

Pressing his cheek against Alice's, Dylan squeezed his eyes shut, holding back his emotions. He'd seen Alice again. He'd touched her and loved her. Come deep inside her. Maybe even if he couldn't clear his name and had to leave this fool town again, she'd have his baby to remember him by.

Maybe.

But now, after he got a little sleep, he had to leave her again.

IN THE DREAM, Dylan was swinging. He was staring down, flying toward the ground, the dew-wet, fresh-cut grass rushing up. The spring breeze cooled his cheeks, flapped in his ears and whisked his golden-blond hair straight back, away from his face.

"You get everything," the voice beside him shouted. "I don't get anything. They hate me."

"Do not," Dylan said.

"Do, too."

"Do not."

Turning his head toward the other swing, Dylan looked at the boy who'd spoken. But he saw only himself—his own soft brown eyes and fine, straight golden hair. He was wearing a paisley button-down shirt that was tucked into black corduroy slacks.

Squinting, he wondered how he could be swinging and, at the same time, be watching himself swing.

The other boy, who also seemed to be Dylan, said, "Push off now," and somehow, even though the words weren't menacing, the tone sent a chill through Dylan. Curling his hands tightly around the chains linking the swing to the bar above, he held on tightly as the ground came closer. Vertigo made his heart race. Stretching his dangling feet, he ran along the ground—one step. Two steps. He pushed off again, his calves tensing as the swing lifted him toward the cloudless, cerulean sky. Then he stopped—right in midair—feeling weightless.

And *whoosh.*

He was falling back down again, moving backward through tunneling air, his hair blowing into his eyes. And then he saw the unbroken, dark surface of the lake.

The lake!

Suddenly everything changed. He wasn't swinging anymore. He was plunging into the water. A hand splashed beneath the surface, grabbed his neck and pushed him down.

He tried running along the lake's bottom—the water was shallow—but he only stirred the sandy bottom. Sand particles and pebbles swirled up. He was freezing—icy cold—but he managed to thrust a soaked shirtsleeve up, above the surface of the water. As it came back down, the sleeve filled with air, ballooning as he clawed at the viselike hand around his neck.

The person wouldn't let go.

His lungs were burning. The icy water was flooding his lungs. The hand on his neck tightened. And tightened. A strange calm descended. Through the water, Dylan saw sunlight. Foliage, too—a lace canopy of treetops.

And a face. Above him, eyes stared curiously down. And then the face swam closer, almost to the water's surface, until it was only inches away.

But that face—the face above him that connected to the hand that clutched his throat—was his own face.

Dylan's eyes fluttered open. His heart was pounding, and his mind was flooded with dream-images. With concentrated effort, he stilled his body, slowed his breathing and relaxed his muscles. His eyes slid across the bed, to where Alice slept. He barely remembered them coming in here. He'd kissed her as they'd come up the steps, and then they'd collapsed. Now he felt exhausted—from the day, from missing her, from their lovemaking.

Damn. He'd sworn to himself he wouldn't sleep long. But the deep slumber had taken him, coming as silently as still lake waters. It slipped over his consciousness, submerging him in darkness. At least he hadn't awakened Alice. The nightmare must have made him toss and turn, but she'd remained as still as a painting, lost to her own dreams.

Or memories.

His still-naked body was drenched in sweat, though the room was cold. Downstairs, the fire in the wood burner was probably low. It was nearly light outside. Through the window, barely visible shapes—leafless tree branches—moved like talons, clawing at the emerging gray, snowy morning. He couldn't see any lights from the main house through the trees.

He glanced at the bedside clock. Only seven. It felt later. He felt as if he'd slept for years. Glancing at Alice again, he hated himself for what he'd just done. He never should have left the hospital with her. Oh, he loved her. Always had, always would. He still wanted her, too. He'd like nothing more than to pull her warm body close and love her again.

Instead, he shuddered. Silently, he crossed his arms over his powerful chest, and wondered what to do. For years, that damn lake had haunted him. He'd seen it in dreams and nightmares. At odd times, visions of it would drift into his mind. He'd see those swings, the still lake's surface and the oleander.

But he'd never thought it was real. Not until tonight. He still couldn't believe how he'd felt when he'd seen it on TV—both relieved and scared. After all these years, he'd realized that his dream-place wasn't a figment of childhood imagination.

And it was a murder site.

A warning chill crept down Dylan's back, and he tried not to imagine how Lang Devlyn had fled his killer. He'd trailed blood from one room to the next, the newscaster had said. Dylan took a steadying breath. At least he now knew the property was real, and that it belonged to Lang Devlyn. *Had* belonged to him, anyway.

Dylan looked over at Alice once more. As he watched her sleep, his mind slipped back to years ago, when he'd first met her. He remembered being outside the general store, sitting in his mother's beat-up Chevy, humming along with Sugarloaf's song, "Green-Eyed Lady." At nothing more than the fullness of the memory, his heart pulled. The day had been so pretty, so warm. And despite what had happened to them since, he could still marvel at the innocence he'd felt back then. Not to mention the faith that everything would come out right in the end.

"Hey," Alice had said, trying to talk without exposing the new braces on her teeth, which had so obviously embarrassed her. "Did anybody ever tell you you look like Lang Devlyn?"

Lang Devlyn.

Dylan did bear a striking resemblance to the man. Staring into the dark, he wondered what his life had to do with Lang Devlyn's. What, if anything, was his connection to the murdered man? Had Dylan really been to the estate he'd seen on TV? Or had he just seen pictures of it in a book about Hollywood?

And if he did have a connection to the music producer, did he also have a connection to the man's murder? Hell, Dylan's memory of the last year and a half was so disjointed. Everything had been nuts. As they said, truth was stranger than fiction. He'd felt so foggy sometimes that he'd actually lost days. He'd chalked it up to fear and depression. After the trauma of being attacked in the church, he'd been living in a haze, totally cut off from everyone and everything

he'd always known and loved, making plans to return
and set things right.

Which was why he had to leave Alice now, even
if it broke his heart. Silently, he drew back the covers
and slipped from bed.

For a long moment, he stood there naked, gazing
down at her. He tried memorizing her face, as if he
didn't already know every inch of it—its creamy skin,
her eyes with their sparse lashes and sandy eyebrows.
Gazing at her, feeling the aching tug of his emotions,
he realized again that he'd never actually told her it
was him.

It's all right. She knows.

That was his last thought as he turned to go.

Chapter Seven

"Where do you think you're going?" Alice asked, wondering how Dylan could come to the cottage, offer her no explanations about the past, make love to her and just leave. Stopping him in the living room, she summed up all her unspoken questions by saying, "How could you?"

"Please." His voice was deceptively soft. His hand was on the doorknob, his eyes holding more dispassion than she could stand. "Just let me go."

"Just let you go?" she echoed, feeling uncharacteristically irrational and ready to go to any lengths to keep him there. "You've only got a few dollars—" Her voice trembled. "No place to go."

"Don't worry about me."

That he didn't want her to made her feel even shakier. So did his brown eyes, which held new resourcefulness, watchful determination and an almost criminal hardness. That wasn't all that was criminal, either. No woman in her right mind could keep her eyes off his body.

An hour later, after the exchange, Alice was still

thinking about Dylan's wanting to leave. Somehow—how she'd never know—she'd gotten him to stay, and now he was in the shower. No doubt, he'd want to leave after that.

When the doorbell rang, she glanced anxiously from the closed bathroom door to the stairs. In the wintry silence, she could still hear the shower running. Surely she could leave him long enough to answer the door. But maybe not. Maybe he'd somehow sneak out of the house.

Swallowing hard, she glanced between the bathroom door and the stairs again. Scenes from countless movies flashed through her mind, where characters left the shower running while they made getaways. Dylan could so easily swing out of an upstairs window, into the waiting branches of a snow-laden tree. He'd climb down, leap to the ground and...

Leave me.

Well, if he wanted to, he would, and there wasn't anything she could do about it. Now that she knew he was alive, now that she'd held him again and they'd made love, she felt almost pathetic in her need to cling. And she still desperately wanted answers about their wedding day. Not that posting herself in front of the bathroom door and standing vigil while he showered was making her feel any less foolish. *If he wants to leave so badly, then let him.*

The doorbell pealed again, this time with a more insistent double ring. Blowing out a sigh, she headed downstairs. Love wasn't supposed to be this way. No, it was supposed to be like...

Like...

Shutting her eyes for a second, she allowed herself to recall every inch of the body she'd held last night. Both her hands and heart had remembered every inch of Dylan: not just the dips and curves of his chest and smooth shoulders, but also the way he'd moved against her. And inside her. Even now, the recollections brought emotional and physical pangs of longing. The changes in him were so remarkable, and yet she knew he was the same man. He still had all that tangled golden hair curling between his pectorals, which was so unlike the black hair on his head that he'd obviously dyed.

"It's probably Mom," she whispered, wondering who was at the door. Or Leland, looking for a repeat of last night's arguments. Or maybe one of the cowhands, bringing information about possible summer rentals for the ranch's guest cottages.

Not that Alice really cared who it was. She didn't have time for visitors. She needed time alone—with Dylan. He hadn't yet told her how he'd made himself look so physically different, or why he'd chosen this particular time to return to Rock Canyon. Was it because he'd known she'd been about to marry Leland? Her heart clutched. She wanted—no, needed—the opportunity to explain why she'd considered doing so. There was so much she and Dylan needed to talk about. And yet, they'd exchanged so few words....

Crimson heat flooded her cheeks as she thought about what they *had* exchanged. Enough to know, beyond a shadow of a doubt, that the man in her shower really was Dylan. She'd recognized his body, and now the heat burning her cheeks spread through the rest of her.

Pausing before the front door, she glanced through the peephole. "Sheriff Sawyer," she whispered dryly. It wasn't her mother, after all. She should have known. Why did the sheriff have to show up now? Why couldn't he have waited an hour or two? Just until she'd talked to Dylan?

If I ever get a chance!

Standing with her hand on the doorknob, Alice wondered again why Dylan had stayed. He hadn't said. He'd merely surveyed her a long moment, then stepped away from the door and headed for the shower.

"I almost wish he hadn't come back." The unexpected words came on a bitter sigh. As much as she loved him, he owed her answers, and he didn't seem very inclined to talk. At moments, she felt as if he'd appeared simply to torture her. And frankly, she'd had enough torture during the past year and a half.

"All right," she muttered when the doorbell rang again. Swinging the door open, she found herself face-to-face with the sheriff.

"'Morning," she said noncommittally. As a rush of biting air tunneled through the open doorway, blowing her hair and stinging her cheeks, she suddenly wished she'd showered. Her hair was held back with two barrettes, and she'd thrown on rumpled maroon sweatpants and a matching sweatshirt. She looked like hell. Somehow, being better dressed might have made it easier to stand her ground. Still, she wasn't about to invite the sheriff inside, not after their exchange last night.

He seemed to know it. He merely surveyed her, his bulky frame filling the doorway. His dark, suspicious eyes darted past her, probing every nook and cranny of the living room. Her eyes drifted over his red down vest pulled over a red-and-black plaid flannel shirt, then stopped on a small light blue nylon sports bag. Its strap was looped over the sheriff's shoulder.

His eyes returned to hers. "Mind if I come in?"

She glanced over her shoulder and listened for the shower, which she was glad to hear was still running. "Sorry," she said. "I wish you'd called. This really isn't the best time."

He pulled on a pair of black leather driving gloves, appraising her all the while. "Is he still here?"

She shot him an innocent look. "Mr. Gerald Williams, you mean?"

"Yeah," the sheriff said softly, his breath fogging the air. "Mr. Williams. Who the hell else would I mean, Alice?"

She didn't bother to keep the animosity from her voice. "He's here, but he's in the shower."

The sheriff's grimly pursed lips said he'd had enough of her shenanigans. "Alice, would you please let me in? I need to talk to that fellow."

"He's unavailable. And," she couldn't help adding, "I don't think I much care for your tone."

He arched an eyebrow. "Well, guess what?"

"What, sheriff?"

"I don't much *care* if you like my tone."

"Please," she said, determined to keep the conversation somewhere in the ballpark of amicable. "I'm very sorry, but I happen to be busy right now."

Rocking back on the heels of his cowboy boots, he gave her the once-over. "Yeah," he said, drawing out the word. "It sure looks like you've been busy."

His suddenly hooded eyes made clear exactly what he thought she'd been busy doing. Hot temper coursed through her. "Do you really think that such a remark will convince me to invite you inside my house?"

"Who knows? It might. You did invite a complete stranger inside, so there's no telling what motivates you."

"Keep it up—" she shot him a tight smile "—and you might even rate some home-cooked muffins and coffee, too."

Her sarcasm only made him livid. "I need to come in," he said flatly.

She returned his stare. "Is that right? What for?"

"To question your houseguest."

The bitter biting wind was blowing right through her sweatsuit, and she clamped her teeth together for an instant, to stop them from chattering. "Do you have a warrant?"

"No, I don't have a warrant! Dammit, Alice, I don't need a warrant to come in your house! I know you!"

"And that means you can ignore people's civil rights?"

"Civil rights!" Sheriff Sawyer fumed. "Have you lost your mind? We've got an unsolved murder in this town. And I want to know who that man is." Poking a finger past her, the sheriff pointed toward the living room.

She said, "Does Mr. Williams need a lawyer?"

"No!" the sheriff snapped.

She shrugged, wishing she wasn't about to freeze to death. "Then I'll bring him down to your office when he's out of the shower." She glanced down. "And after I'm more appropriately dressed."

The sheriff's eyes slid past her again, into the living room. He glanced up the stairs. "Just what do you think is in here?" she said haughtily. *Murdered bodies? A murder weapon?*

"You know," he said, "for the record, I've got to say that I don't like your attitude."

"I didn't like yours when you all but convicted Dylan," she returned.

"You've already told me, Alice. Many times."

As far as she was concerned, he had yet to hear it enough. "Well, now you've heard it again."

Blowing out a murderous sigh, he shoved his hands on his hips. "Can you bring him down in the next couple of hours?" Before she could answer, he all but thrust the blue nylon bag at Alice. "Here. Clarisse down at the Blue Sage Motel in town ID'd Mr. Williams from the Polaroids I took at the hospital. Clarisse said he was carrying this bag when he checked into the motel. Said he paid cash and—"

"You had no right to take pictures!" Alice exclaimed, her mind catching up. She should have known better than to leave Dylan with the sheriff. "He, uh, Mr. Williams is not suspected of any crime, which means you don't have any right—"

"We've already been over this, Alice. I have every right." The sheriff's eyes became dark beady points. "Why do you care about this man, anyway? And I still want to know why you called him Dylan."

That was one question she'd rather not answer. Instead she straightened and said, "Now, Sheriff, I want you off my porch!" She knew she was making even more of an enemy out of Sheriff Sawyer, but she wasn't letting him question Dylan before she did.

"Go ahead," the sheriff said. "Keep locking horns with me, girl, and see where that gets you and your...friend." He said the word as if it were something dirty, his eyes dropping slowly over her. "Rest assured, Alice," he finally continued, "I'm keeping tabs on you. And I expect you to bring that man down to my office within the next two hours."

She was starting to feel downright sullen. "I said I'd have him there, didn't I? I have to drive to the hospital and pick up my paycheck, anyway."

"You bring him in," the sheriff said succinctly, "whether you have anywhere else to go or not."

"Judge, jury and executioner," she said. "You're treating this man the same way you treated Dylan. When are you going to start acting like a sheriff again?"

"When my daughter's murder is solved."

Her heart thudded. And she hated herself for pushing him so far. But didn't he understand that his obsession with Jan's murder had pushed him *away* from solving it?

The sheriff's eyes were now as dark as coals. "Alice," he said, "it might be wise to remember that you were the intended murder victim."

A shudder rippled through her. "That was never proved."

"Lying there, Jan looked just like you. And she was wearing your wedding veil."

Guilt flooded her. What if he was right? What if she, not Jan, was supposed to have died? "That doesn't mean I was the intended victim."

"Think about it."

She was. She remembered running her hand over the blood-covered white dress, trying desperately to staunch the countless wounds. In that second, she'd realized how much she and Jan looked alike. *Someone wanted to kill me,* she had thought.

Now words from the phone call she'd received yesterday played in her head, and she felt faint. *She bled like a pig. And you know what, Alice? I thought she was you. I said to myself, "Dylan, you're going to cut your pretty little wife."* Feeling sick, she realized the sheriff was still glaring at her. Why couldn't he just leave her alone? She wanted to sink back inside, where the fire was warm.

"If you want to protect this man, this stranger, then that's fine," the sheriff was saying. "But by the end of the day, I'll probably know whether or not he's really Gerald Williams. If the man's got any kind of record, which most vagrants do, then I'll definitely know who he is, since we're running his prints."

She gasped. "You can't fingerprint a man without cause! When did you—"

This time, the sheriff didn't smile. "At the hospital when you left the room to get coffee."

Her heart started beating too fast. Back in high school, a bunch of the popular guys—Dylan included—had pulled a typically juvenile prank and run naked down Main Street after a regional basketball playoff. The boys had been charged, fingerprinted and sentenced to four Saturdays of community service. No doubt the prints were still on file. Which meant Sheriff Sawyer would soon find out that the man upstairs was Dylan Nolan.

Terror coursed through her. Realizing how carefully the sheriff was watching her, she did her best to mask her emotions. "You had no right to fingerprint him," she argued righteously, with more confidence than she felt. "He committed no crime."

The sheriff's smile didn't meet his eyes. "Last night, the man was unnamed, unconscious, and he'd been hit by a car—"

"*Your* car," she reminded him.

He nodded. "Exactly. Given the circumstances, I was within my legal bounds. Now, Alice," he continued, almost drawling the words, "when it comes to legal bounds, you'd just better make sure that you're within yours."

She was getting furious. "Meaning?"

"You know what I mean."

Unfortunately, she did. She was hiding pertinent information. And the sheriff was no fool.

"And, Alice?"

She glanced up, meeting his eyes. "What?"

"One more thing." The sheriff jerked his head,

drawing her attention to the county car in her driveway. For the first time, she realized Leland was here.
She'd been so intent on the sheriff that she hadn't
noticed Leland leaning against the driver's-side door,
facing her house.

She stared at Leland a long moment.

He stared back, not moving. His arms remained
crossed over his chest, and his long, lanky jeans-clad
legs were crossed at the ankles. Even though light
flurries fell and snow from the drifts blew, he stood
there, slowly, thoughtfully pulling at his mustache.

"Leland," the sheriff said softly, "is going to be
watching you, too."

It sounded like a threat. Her eyes shifted from Leland to the sheriff. "What's between me and Leland
doesn't concern you, Sheriff Sawyer."

The sheriff didn't look convinced. "Oh," he said
as he turned to go, "absolutely everything in this
town concerns me, Alice. 'Sides, Leland's a pretty
angry young man." The sheriff shot her a smile.
"Which means he's highly motivated to help me figure out why you're so cozy with that fellow in there."

Cozy. She started to defend herself, but they'd been
cozy, all right. And the sudden, bright color burning
in her cheeks was the admission of it. Not that it
mattered. The sheriff had already turned away. Warily, Alice watched him make his way down the shov-
eled stone path to the driveway. Without offering her
so much as another glance, Leland circled the car, got
in and slammed the door.

Everything seemed strangely silent. Too silent. And
then Alice realized the shower had quit running. Her

heart pounded with panic, and before she even realized she was doing it, she slammed the front door
shut, whirled around and ran upstairs. Stopping
breathlessly in front of the bathroom door, she realized she was still clutching the nylon bag the sheriff
had given her. Her tone was sharper than she intended. ''Are you in there?''

No answer. Then a gruff, ''Yes.''

Turning abruptly, she headed back downstairs. She
started to put another log into the wood burner, but
there wasn't time. Glancing guiltily toward the stairs,
she tossed the bag onto the couch. Well, if he caught
her going through his things, too bad, she thought.
She had every right to seek answers, didn't she? Sitting down, she opened the bag's zipper and rummaged inside, finding a pair of jeans, a couple of
shirts...

She frowned. Something was wrong.

Staring into the bag, she wasn't sure why she
thought so. Nor did she fully understand what possessed her to grab Dylan's clothes and bring them to
her nose. She inhaled. Strange, but the clothes didn't
smell like Dylan. Alice shook her head and kept rum-
maging.

''Nothing,'' she muttered, glancing nervously toward the stairs again. ''What did you expect?'' No
doubt the cops had been through everything here.

There were socks. A couple pairs of briefs, though
last night, Dylan had been wearing—and had always
worn—boxers. Suddenly, she saw something drop;
gold flashed from the hem of a shirt to the couch. Her
eyes settling on a chain, she dug both hands between

the couch cushions until her fingers closed around something flat and round, like a coin.

She gasped. Years ago she'd given this medallion to Dylan. For a second she clutched it to her chest, holding it over her heart. Wherever Dylan had gone, he'd taken this with him, and just the thought filled her with warmth and joy.

Finally, real proof that the man upstairs was Dylan.

Lovingly she ran her thumbnail around the locket, finding the catch. But when it fell open, her heart turned to ice. Inside was her picture. She remembered it well—a black-and-white studio picture of her, wearing a plain black off-the-shoulder dress with a single strand of pearls.

But now little pinpricks dotted her face. It was as if someone had repeatedly stabbed the tiny picture with a knife. And across the picture, written in red letters—so small she could barely read them—it said, *See her bleed.*

Chapter Eight

See her bleed. The words were still playing in Alice's head when LaVryle said, "Sure, I'll get your paycheck for you, hon."

"Thanks, LaVryle." Alice glanced anxiously toward the corridor, as if Dylan might appear. Would the man really stay in the front lobby, where she'd left him? Or would he use this opportunity to vanish?

Alice looked at LaVryle again. Usually, nothing more than watching the older woman could lighten Alice's mood, but now she had to force a smile as the head of personnel rummaged through a desk drawer. LaVryle was definitely something to behold; at less than five feet tall and carrying more than a few extra pounds, she was well past retirement age, and yet every inch of her girth still communicated an enviable love of life.

Alice wasn't feeling quite so positive at the moment.

"Darn if your check isn't still locked up in that safe," LaVryle said. Licking the remnants of a chocolate cookie from her fingertips, she hopped up from her desk. As she crossed the office, the western-style boots protruding from under her jean skirt made sharp clicks on the tile floor. "Be right back."

"Thanks," Alice said. "I appreciate it."

As LaVryle disappeared into an adjacent room, Alice caught a glimpse of her own reflection in the doorway's glass. She'd smoothed her hair, pulling the blond strands back with ivory barrettes, and she'd donned her best brown wool slacks and a camel blazer. Amazing. How could she look so well put together under the circumstances?

Alice just wished things were as fine as the picture she presented, but the locket tucked in her blazer pocket was a reminder of the truth. Her fingers trembled as she traced the smooth, cool metal, and she inhaled sharply, hoping to quiet the unexpectedly rapid beat of her heart. Earlier, seeing her own defiled picture had left her so terrified that she hadn't even heard Dylan come downstairs. She'd still been registering the horrible chicken-scratched letters written in bloodred, while her eyes roved over the knife pricks marring her face.

See her bleed.

See her bleed.

See her bleed.

The words kept turning in her mind like a broken record. And then the deeper thought. *Oh, God. Someone wants to kill me.*

"See her bleed." Alice now caught herself mouthing those sick, vile words, as if forming them with her lips would make them seem more real. It didn't. Was this really happening? she wondered in panic.

Did someone—maybe even Dylan—want to harm her? To kill her? And why? What had she ever done to hurt anyone? Growing up, she'd always been a good girl. She'd been nice to people. Made a lot of friends.

Earlier today, coming from the stairs, Dylan's voice had startled her. "What's that?"

Her heart pounding, Alice had realized he'd stopped at the entrance to the living room. "Nothing," she'd managed to say, avoiding his eyes as she impulsively shoved the locket down between the couch cushions again. She'd tried to steady the tremor in her voice. "It's just your bag. The sheriff got it from the motel where you were staying, and he dropped it by."

Dylan stared at the bag as if he'd never seen it before, and somehow, the disturbed puzzlement in his gaze made her heart race—and made her persist. "The desk clerk said you were carrying this bag when you checked in."

There was no response, only another slight widening of Dylan's eyes.

"What?" she'd demanded sharply. *Why are you looking at the bag like that?* Why did he look so scared? Or at least as close to scared as such a self-possessed man could look.

He'd run a hand raggedly through his wavy black hair and shrugged. "Nothing." There was a twinge of irony in his voice. "It's just awful nice of the sheriff to drop by with my things."

If it was Dylan's bag, why had he looked at it so suspiciously? Blowing out another anxious sigh, Alice wished Dylan would talk to her. She'd tried again, but he'd merely watched her, his eyes too hard to read. She definitely had to get some answers before Sheriff Sawyer questioned him.

Especially now that she'd seen the locket. That changed everything. Dylan could never hurt her, so there had to be some explanation for what had been done to her picture.

Glancing around the personnel office, her heart hammered. Adorned with lively children's artwork and fresh flowers, the office was so...nice. Just like all of Rock Canyon. At least on the surface. Alice thought of Main Street's clean sidewalks, well-lit stores and country-style restaurants.

Dammit. It was all such a lie: her nice clothes, the bright, cheerful office, the town in which she lived. Beneath the surface, Alice had glimpsed too many other things. Jan Sawyer in a pool of her own blood. And Nancy Nolan's beaten, unconscious body stretched on a hospital bed, hooked to monitors. And now, finally, a locket containing Alice's own defiled picture.

See me bleed.

Alice shuddered. After finding the locket, she'd tried to get Dylan to talk, but she'd been too scared to push him. Lord, what if he *had* meant to kill her on their wedding day? And what if he'd killed Jan? Did their marriage really make him go crazy, somehow, the way some people had claimed it did?

But no, Alice couldn't believe such things of Dylan.

And yet ever since she'd found the locket, a horrible feeling of foreboding had threatened to over-whelm her. She felt sure that Jan's murder was about to be rehashed, somehow.

Or reenacted.

Lord, what if he'd come back to torture her, to toy with her like a mouse? *Quit thinking like this, Alice! Are you crazy?* She firmly pushed aside the fears. If she began doubting Dylan now, they'd both be lost.

"Oh, c'mon, LaVryle," she muttered nervously, turning her gaze to a window. Outside, the hospital grounds seemed unnervingly quiet, like a menacing still life. Hard to believe her world had once been all summers and sunshine. Now it seemed so dark, so touched by evil. Unbidden, the dead rock-icon, Lang Devlyn, entered her thoughts. Had it been this way for him, too? In his last moments, had the old man wondered at his own fall from grace? Had he remem-bered his innocent, smiling fans as he crawled from room to room in his mansion? How long had he trailed smears across marble floors, slowly bleeding to death, before he realized his attempts to evade his killer were utterly futile?

See him bleed.

A slow chill crept down Alice's spine. Her eyes continued scanning the grounds. Why, she didn't know. What, exactly, was she searching for? Maybe for some reassuring sign of life—some birds or a squirrel—but there was nothing. Not even wind touched the barren, snow-blanketed ground.

"Don't spend it all in one place!"

Alice gasped, startled. Clamping a hand over her heart, she drew in a quick breath. "Thanks, La-

Vryle.'' Her fingers trembling, she took the envelope containing her paycheck.

"You all right?'' LaVryle peered at her. "You're shaking like a leaf.''

"Sure,'' Alice murmured. "Guess I'm just cold.'' *Cold in such a soul-deep way that I feel like I'll never get warm again.*

"Yep, it's colder'n a witch's you-know-what!'' LaVryle announced, then she shrugged. "Oh, c'mon, Alice. Confide in old LaVryle. Everybody knows you and Leland didn't get married yesterday. And the nurses from the third floor said you took home some vagrant who was brought into the ER last night. Not that anybody blames you. Fact is, they were green as grass with envy. Every darn gal on the night shift agreed he was the best-looking fellow to ever get hit by a car in Rock Canyon. They're glad to know he's fine, too. Nevertheless, we are all dying to know who he is.''

Dying? I'm the one who might be dying. Oh, LaVryle, I'm going crazy, and I can't talk about it, but I think someone wants me dead.

Not that Alice could say that, since it would also mean divulging the "vagrant's'' real identity. God only knew what would happen if people realized the stranger was Dylan. There'd be a lynch mob, no doubt headed by Sheriff Sawyer. Alice was still searching for an appropriate response, when LaVryle continued, "While I was fetching your check, another nurse called. She says you brought that man back here today, that he's up in Nancy Nolan's room right now, sitting next to her on the bed and talking to her as if he's her long-lost kin.''

"He's in Nancy's room?" Alice said, foreboding shooting through her. She'd left him in the lobby! What if Dylan really *had* attacked his mother, the way some people assumed? She didn't actually believe it, but she had to consider it. What if he was in his mother's room now, getting ready to hurt her again?

"Alice?"

Her heart was racing. "Sorry, LaVryle. I've got to go."

Bolting for the elevator, Alice realized her fingers felt frozen, like ice. Folding her paycheck, she shoved it into her pocket, next to the locket.

As the elevator ascended, she didn't take her eyes from the lit-up numbers overhead, not until it reached Nancy's floor.

At Nancy's doorway, Alice released an inaudible sigh of relief. Nothing was amiss. Only now did she realize just how hard her heart was pounding. Lord, had she really expected to find Nancy dead and Dylan gone? She shook her head, dispelling the confusion. She had to get a grip. To stick to the facts and reality. Dylan was no more capable of murder than she was, and she couldn't let her imagination get the best of her.

Dylan hadn't yet heard her. Seated on the edge of Nancy's bed, he leaned close, holding one of Nancy's pale lifeless hands between both of his. He was talking—uttering a slow, steady stream of words—but his voice was such a low murmur that Alice couldn't tell what he was saying. Listening to the seductive rumble, she heard the tender emotion, though, and her heart did a jittery flip-flop. She didn't know what was happening here, but how could she doubt this man? Ever since she'd found that locket, her emotions had seesawed.

As she took another tentative step inside the room, her fingers grazed the locket in her pocket again. Just the touch of it made her heart thud harder. The locket seemed like a living thing, and her whole body absorbed the cold chill of its metal. She kept eyeing Dylan. She was so tired of asking him what was going on. Every time she did, he offered nothing. And, if the truth be told, maybe she was afraid of the answers he'd give. Just how scary was the truth?

She crept closer.

Suddenly his head jerked toward her, and he stared at her, slack-jawed. His voice was a gruff accusation. "You scared the hell out of me."

"Why, Dylan? What are you afraid of?"

He still didn't affirm or deny that was his name; he only glanced away and disentangled his hand from his mother's.

There was a long silence. Alice tried not to notice how everything in the room seemed so deathly white—the sheets, the hospital gown, the walls, the floor. Nancy Nolan's chalky face.

Not that Nancy had looked this way when she was first brought to the hospital. Even now, Alice shuddered to think of what Nancy's attacker had done to her. When Alice had first visited, she hadn't even recognized her mother-in-law. Nancy's lips were cracked and swollen, her skin dark with bruises. One eye drooped, the other was swollen shut.

Seeing the damage, Alice had been sure Sheriff Sawyer was wrong. No mere robber did that kind of damage to a woman. The man—no, monster—had wanted something more...to hurt this beautiful woman, to mar her lovely face.

To see her bleed.

"Look," Alice found herself saying to Dylan, mustering all her courage. "We need to talk. I...found something earlier." She paused, swallowing hard. "Something disturbing..."

His eyes narrowed, the brown irises looking darker in the low light. "Disturbing?"

She nodded, her heart beating so hard that she could hear it pounding in her ears. "Yes..."

His lips parted. He was about to say something more, when an out-of-sequence beep sounded from Nancy's monitors. Then came a quicker succession. *Beep-beep-beep. Beep-beep-beep.* Turning, Alice gasped. "Oh, God, her eyelids!" They were fluttering.

Suddenly, Nancy Nolan's eyes were flung wide open. She gasped—a harsh, suffocating inhalation.

Grabbing the call button, Alice rang, even though the monitors were being read from the nurse's station. "Take it easy," she told her, her own heart racing. It wasn't every day that a comatose patient awakened; these first moments were crucial.

From down the hallway, footsteps pounded, coming closer.

Dylan's voice caught. "Is she all right?"

Alice barely felt him beside her as she ministered to Nancy, adjusting the woman's IV's. "I don't know."

"What can I do?"

"Nothing."

"Alice," a nurse said from the doorway. "You're here."

Alice gave her a quick nod. "Is Dr. Macintosh in the hospital?"

"Sure is."

"Page him. She's stable. I'll stay."

The nurse took off. Even as Alice checked the dilation of Nancy's pupils, she realized that the eyes held sheer terror. The trauma of awakening, Alice thought.

But it was more. Nancy wasn't darting her eyes around the room to get her bearings. She seemed to know exactly where she was. And who she was looking at.

Dylan.

She was staring at him. Of course she recognized him, Alice thought. A mother always knew her son. But suddenly, with superhuman effort, Nancy lifted her hand. Clawing the air, she clutched Alice's fingers, drawing Alice close. "Don't try to talk," Alice murmured. "You'll be fine. Your doctor's on his way. Don't use up your strength."

Nancy's rasp came from a bone-dry throat. "Be..." Even with her ear to Nancy's mouth, Alice could barely hear. "Care...ful."

Tingles slid down Alice's spine.

"Son...tried...to kill me."

Alice was still registering the words when Dr. Macintosh flew into the room, and pushed her away from
Nancy. A second later, Dylan's words sounded so
close to Alice's ear that tingles of an altogether different kind coursed through her body. His voice was
soft, insistent. "What did she say, Alice?"

Alice glanced up. Unbidden, she thought of the
phone call she'd received, the locket and Nancy's
warning. Despite the changes in Dylan, his mother
had recognized his eyes. Now, gazing into the brown
depths, Alice didn't know what to believe. Nancy Nolan loved her son. And yet she'd identified him as her
attacker.

Son...tried...to kill me.

Alice suddenly felt nauseated. And so alone. Other
horrible words she'd been privy to in these past
twenty-four hours washed over her once more. *See
her bleed. Want to come through the looking glass,
Alice?*

"Nothing," Alice somehow managed to say. "I—
I tried, but I couldn't make out the words."

LELAND'S VOICE dripped with irony. "Well, howdy
there, Alice. Long time, no see."

Great. This was the last thing she needed. What
happened at the hospital was bad enough. So was
wondering if she was right to maintain her composure
around Dylan. Even worse, Sheriff Sawyer had left
Dylan in an interrogation room because he wanted to
talk with her alone.

And now Leland.

He was leaning against a whitewashed cinder block

wall, between a water fountain and a bulletin board tacked with most-wanted posters, absently tweaking his mustache. He was wearing jeans and a faded denim shirt; his black Stetson was pulled so low over his forehead that Alice could barely see his eyes. Despite his casual stance, his whole body communicated danger. As if Alice hadn't felt enough fear today, between finding the locket and hearing Nancy Nolan's warning.

"Hello, Leland."

The challenge in his eyes made her blood boil every bit as much as the obvious suggestion in his voice. "Have a good time with your new boyfriend last night, Alice?"

She tamped down the unwanted heat that threatened to rise in her cheeks. "Look," she found herself saying, wishing he'd respond to reason, "I'd love to talk, Leland, but—" She jerked her head toward Sheriff Sawyer who was waiting for her inside a conference room.

"But what?" Leland's angry eyes drifted over her. "Too ashamed of your behavior?" Before she could answer, he added, "Hmm. A wayward girl like you…maybe she oughtta be punished."

Her voice was sharp. "A wayward girl like me?" Once more, she felt convinced that Leland's jealousy could have driven him to murder. Had he tried to get Dylan out of the picture so he could marry her?

"That's what I said. Maybe you ought to be punished."

See her bleed. Her eyes narrowed. "Leland, are you threatening me?"

"Take it however you like."

Somehow, she kept her composure. She wished she could talk to the sheriff about how Leland was treating her. And about Leland's claims that he hadn't loved Jan. Not that she could tell Jan's father that. "When you cool off, we'll talk."

He crossed his arms, making the rolled-up sleeves of his denim shirt pull so tight over his corded forearms that she half thought the fabric would rip. "Sorry," he said in a deceptively soft drawl. "I do believe I've had just about all the talking I can stand. Fact is, I've got better things to do than talk."

"Then what are you hanging around here for?" she returned with anger that was calculated to mask her fear. When he didn't answer, she glanced through a window at the far end of the hallway. Birds that had been perched in a stark-looking barren tree suddenly took flight, scattering into the sky. Something had startled them. Damn if Alice didn't know the feeling. "Look, Leland," she continued, turning back to him and feeling determined not to let him see her fear. "The fact is, you *do* have better things to take care of today."

Again that deceptively lazy voice rolled over her ears. "You mean besides tailing you, Alice?"

Her pulse quickened. It figured. All morning, she could swear someone was watching her, though she'd written off the feeling to her own suppressed anxiety. At the thought of Leland's spying, she felt another rush of anger. "Yes," she returned, surprised to hear how even her voice sounded. "You should be running the ranch. My family pays you good money to do your job." *The job that was Dylan's before he vanished.*

Leland leveled her with a dark stare. "Too bad. I quit."

"What?" She couldn't believe this. Leland had worked the Eastman ranch since he was a teenager, and he'd been overseeing things since Dylan disappeared. Which meant Dylan's disappearance had translated into a big promotion for Leland, too. While both boys had started working the ranch when they were sixteen, Alice's dad had always said Dylan was quicker than Leland, that he had a natural way with cattle. Not to mention a better head for numbers. Exactly how angry was Leland about the fact that Dylan had gotten what Leland most wanted—a position running the largest ranch in this part of Wyoming....

And my love.

Alice swallowed hard and looked at Leland one last time. "If that's what you want," she found herself saying. She couldn't keep the sudden haughtiness from her voice. "Whenever you decide you want to have a real conversation with me, you just let me know." With that, she strode into the conference room, her gaze now settling on Sheriff Sawyer who loudly shut the door behind her.

Alice glanced toward a two-way mirror that looked into the interrogation room where Dylan waited. Dylan gazed back at her through the glass. Obviously he knew the mirror into which he was staring did a heck of a lot more than reflect his good looks.

Watching him, Alice wished for the umpteenth time that he wasn't so hard to read. Or that she knew how much to say—or leave unsaid. Was she in danger from him, or not? She looked at the sheriff. "What is it you want to say to me that you can't say in front of that man?"

Sheriff Sawyer thrust a stubby-fingered hand through his thick silver hair. "Dammit, Alice. As an old family friend, I'm giving you one last chance to talk. I still want to know why you called him Dylan last night."

"And I want to know why you put him in that interrogation room," she retorted. "Need I remind you he's here of his own volition? Which means, at the very least, he should be in your private office, comfortably drinking a cup of hot coffee."

Sheriff Sawyer rolled his eyes. "Gee," he returned dryly. "Maybe he'd like to sample some of our jelly-filled doughnuts, too."

"The offer would have been hospitable."

The sheriff's eyes narrowed. "One more time, Alice. Are you going to tell me why you called that man Dylan?"

"I've told you. I don't know why. Maybe wishful thinking."

The sheriff was scrutinizing her. Obviously he knew there was more to it. "Like I said, this is your last chance."

She raised an eyebrow. "What are you going to do? Arrest me?"

"You'd better believe it," he returned. "If I find out you're withholding information, it'll be the least I do."

"I'm scared."

"You should be, girl."

Suddenly she swallowed hard. Oh, she didn't much like Sheriff Sawyer, not after the way he'd handled the investigation into Jan's murder. But maybe he was right. She shoved her hands in the pockets of her camel blazer. The locket was still there, next to her folded paycheck, its metal surface feeling as smooth and cold as the paper envelope. She felt a warning tremor in her throat. "Please," she managed to say levelly. "I've said everything I intend to. Now, can we just get this over with?"

"Your pleasure. You can wait for him in the lobby."

Her lips parted in astonishment. "No way." She jerked her head toward Dylan. "I'm going to be in that room, watching your every move."

"Whatever." Without another word, Sheriff Sawyer headed for the door. "Just don't say I didn't give you a last chance to come clean with me."

She followed the sheriff into the corridor. "He doesn't need to talk to you," Alice reminded again.

As the sheriff opened the door to the interrogation room, he said, "I'll be the judge of that."

Alice crossed her arms and leaned against the ugly pale pink wall while the sheriff seated himself across from Dylan at the metal table. Hazarding a glance toward the two-way mirror, Alice thought she saw a shadow. So much for civil rights in Rock Canyon. No doubt Leland was in there, watching.

Lord, let's just get this over with. Alice sighed. She was starting to feel downright tired from worry and fear. While she was too afraid to keep pushing Dylan, she wasn't scared enough to confide in the sheriff. Besides, what could she really say? That she'd recognized Dylan's eyes?

You could show Sheriff Sawyer the locket.

The sheriff's voice drew her from her thoughts. He said, "What is it you want?"

Raising a dark eyebrow, Dylan surveyed the sheriff. He didn't fidget, the way most men probably would under such careful scrutiny. Leaning slightly forward, he rested his forearms on the table. "Want?"

"Yeah," the sheriff clarified. "Here, in Rock Canyon."

"To pass through peaceably," Dylan returned. "Like I said, I was down in Cheyenne, and I heard there might be work around these parts."

"Is that right, Mr. Williams? You were down in Cheyenne, huh?"

Dylan nodded. "Sure was, sir."

"Then how do you explain this?" From his vest pocket, the sheriff pulled a small, transparent bag tagged with a neon green evidence sticker. Alice recognized the type of sticker; it was the same kind the police used when they removed items from bodies in the ER. She squinted. Inside the bag was a ticket.

"According to this—" Sheriff Sawyer tossed the bag onto the gray metal table "—you just came from L.A. The ticket was with your bag in the motel room."

"Then you had no right to take it!" Alice said.

The sheriff glared at her. Dylan remained utterly still.

"That's illegal search and seizure!" Alice had no

idea if that was true—she was hardly a lawyer—but it sure seemed as if the sheriff had overstepped his bounds. Of course, he'd probably cover his tracks so he wouldn't get in trouble.

The sheriff was piercing Dylan with another hard stare, which Dylan met dead-on. "Like I said, Alice," the sheriff continued, still looking at Dylan, "I'm within my rights. I know what I'm doing."

"Enough to cover yourself," she muttered.

"Enough of your mouth," warned the sheriff. She glanced at Dylan, who remained expressionless, and she was about to respond, when a sudden knock sounded—three quick raps on the door.

"What?" the sheriff shouted.

The door swung open and Leland's head popped in. He didn't grace her or Dylan with so much as a glance. "Sheriff, you're needed out here. Some stuff just came through that you're gonna be real interested in seeing."

The sheriff glanced between her and Dylan. "Don't either of you two move."

She gave a nod of acquiescence, which was more than Dylan offered as the sheriff left the room. She glanced at Dylan. He met her gaze, his eyes looking dark and thoughtful, but he said nothing. She was determined not to. Why, she didn't know. Maybe out of sheer perversity. If he wanted to play the strong, silent type, fine. She could wait.

It seemed forever before the sheriff reentered the room. When he did, he didn't look good. In fact, he looked older, almost haggard, as if the few minutes away had aged him full years. Alice realized he probably hadn't slept last night. Probably since having a stranger in town put his radar on alert. He'd been sure he'd found a lead to his daughter's murderer. Now his dark eyes seemed to sag, the skin beneath them turning fleshy and slack. Lord, what kind of news had the man just received?

"Nancy?" she couldn't help saying.

"She's fine," the sheriff said gruffly.

"Thank God," Alice said, pressing a hand to her heart. And yet she knew it was only a matter of time until Nancy identified Dylan. Surely, Nancy was wrong.

Sheriff Sawyer reseated himself, then he cleared his throat. "Looks as if we've got some real interesting news." He slid two sheets of fax paper across the table, and Alice stepped closer to get a better look. It was just as she feared. On the pages were fingerprints. She squinted. She'd assumed Dylan's prints were still in the sheriff's files, but this looked more official, like something downloaded from a national database.

"Mr. Devlyn," the sheriff said slowly, his hard, uncompromising eyes settling on Dylan. "I think you'd better start talking. And you might want to begin with what you're really doing in Rock Canyon, Wyoming, carrying a fake ID. With your background, you sure as hell don't need money or a job on a ranch."

For the first time, Dylan spoke. "Did I miss something here?"

The sheriff's voice was level. "I'd like to remind you that you've crossed state lines. We can make a federal case out of this, if we choose."

Devlyn? Edging nearer, Alice continued staring down at the fax. Sure enough, the fingerprints identified this man as someone named Stuart Devlyn!

"Who?" Alice said shakily, her voice sounding strangled to her own ears. "Who did you say he was?"

The sheriff's assessing eyes settled on her, and his lips twisted into a slight smile. "Maybe you'll think twice next time," he said coldly, "before you ask strangers into your home. Your mother's worried sick. She called me this morning. And if your father were still alive, he'd tan your ever-lovin' hide."

Her pulse was racing. She turned her eyes to Dylan. Or to the man she'd *thought* was Dylan, but whose's real name was apparently Stuart Devlyn. He stared back. And that fool face—that devastatingly gorgeous fool face—was every bit as unreadable as it was moments before. Feeling suddenly faint, Alice stepped back again, shrinking against the wall for support.

But those eyes, she thought in panic. *They're Dylan's eyes. I'd know them anywhere. I know I'm not wrong!* What on earth was happening? She knew those beautiful brown eyes the way every woman knew the eyes of her lover. Countless times, she'd seen them spark with honey-gold fire. Or darken with passion, becoming black-streaked, like tiger's-eye stones.

Please, oh please, she thought, her knees weakening. She couldn't have been wrong! She couldn't have allowed a stranger into her home! *Into my bed!* Her throat constricted and fire flooded her cheeks. What could she say now? That she'd only brought this man home because she'd been sure he was Dylan in disguise?

Nothing in the room was moving. Not her. Not Dylan. Not the sheriff.

But suddenly, every inch of her was burning. She tried not to remember the things she'd let him do to her. How he'd ravished her half-clothed until she was hot and damp with sweat and wanting more.

She tried to forget, but in her mind's eye he was jerking down her hose and panties. With a pang, she felt his hard heat thrusting up—against her, in her. Shame coursed through her veins. She'd been so brazen, wrapping her legs around his back, urging him inside her.

Now she felt sick. "Who?" she said hoarsely, the one word reverberating in her ears. *Oh, please,* she thought once more, her mind still unwilling to believe it. *Tell me I didn't make love to a stranger.*

"About time you took some interest in your gentleman caller," the sheriff said dryly. "Restores my faith in the morals of today's youth."

Damn the sheriff. He seemed to be enjoying himself now. And damn Stuart Devlyn, too. Whoever *he* was. She stared at him in shock, her eyes livid with accusation. There wasn't a thing she could say in front of the sheriff. If she did, she'd be admitting she'd thought the man was Dylan. She wasn't about to tell the sheriff that.

But the man had known.

And everything in her piercing stare called him on his deceit. She'd never have slept with him if she hadn't mistaken him for her husband. He knew it, too.

Countless times last night, she'd tried to get him to admit he was Dylan, and now she knew exactly why he hadn't.

Her voice shook. "You say his name's Stuart Devlyn?"

"Stuart Devlyn," the sheriff repeated.

Devlyn. She was still so stunned she couldn't move, but the name tugged at her consciousness. In her stupor, she was only vaguely aware that she'd heard it recently. Where?

Oh God! Images of the Lang Devlyn estate rushed into her mind, and she remembered this man's intent expression as he'd watched reports of the musician's murder. Stuart Devlyn? Lang Devlyn? Surely there was no relation!

Oddly, the man who was apparently Stuart Devlyn looked just as stunned as she did. Very slowly, he lifted the two pages on the table and scrutinized them. "Where did you get these?" he asked.

The voice moved through her, sounding so much like Dylan's. But it was different, too. Deeper and richer. It was as if the last year and a half had made Dylan confront cold hard realities that could be heard when he spoke.

But, of course, this wasn't Dylan!

The sheriff was watching him, just as she was. "Get what?"

"The prints."

"Right off your fingertips, at the hospital last night."

"Impossible," the man muttered.

The sheriff shrugged. "Two of my boys were in the room, and watched the whole process."

The man leveled the sheriff with a steady stare. "You took them off my fingertips?"

The sheriff looked testy. "That's what I just said, Mr. Devlyn."

"Stuart Devlyn," the man repeated, still scrutinizing the papers. "These were on file," he said slowly. "I...don't recall being arrested in the past."

"You weren't." The sheriff looked at him oddly. "Your family wanted prints on file with the police, I guess in case anything ever happened to you. Like kidnapping. I guess it's not uncommon when you're from a prestigious family with money."

"Money?"

"That's right," said the sheriff. "Look, Stuart, we've got some talking to do. First, I still want to know what you're doing in my town with a fake ID that says you're Gerald Williams. Second, you need to return a call to Lieutenant Louie Santiago in Los Angeles, California."

The man still looked surprised. Alice's heart was hammering. So he was from a rich family? And damn the sheriff for suddenly kowtowing to him because he was rich.

He said, "I need to call L.A.?"

The sheriff leaned forward, losing his deferential tone, which Alice was glad of. "I don't know what kind of game you're playing here. Your father was just murdered in L.A. You know that, right?"

The man glanced away, and the faraway look in his eyes reminded Alice of how he'd looked last night, with those eyes glued to the television screen. A shudder went through her as she remembered the scene at Lang Devlyn's estate: the still shot of the quiet lake, the stationary swings. It looked like a dead paradise.

"He was murdered," the man said slowly. "I know that, yes."

"And now it looks as if you hopped on a plane and came here right after it happened," Sheriff Sawyer said. "Not to worry. The Bel-Air P.D. has a lead on someone. But they desperately want to question you. Which means they want you on the very next flight. There's one tomorrow morning that can get you to a connector in Cheyenne. Sorry, but Rock Canyon isn't exactly a hub." The sheriff sighed. "Right now, they want your word you're coming."

"Okay. I'll go."

Sheriff Sawyer stared at him. "You know I'd just as soon hold you. I've got a number of questions, myself."

The man said nothing.

"You'll stay in town tonight?"

The man finally nodded. "If something comes up tonight, I'll be at Alice's."

She gaped at him. This was an outrage! What on earth was happening? Stuart Devlyn, son of a recently slain, once-famous rock icon, had just waltzed into her life. He'd slept with her—and all while he'd known she thought he was another man.

Somehow she found her voice. "I think Mr. Devlyn might find other lodgings for the night."

He said, "Can we discuss this when we're alone?"

"Guess not," she returned, hardly caring that the sheriff was listening. "Because I never intend to be alone with you again." And then, right before she whirled around and slammed through the door, she furiously tossed over her shoulder, "Mr. Devlyn."

Chapter Nine

He wasn't but twenty feet behind her, following her across the ice-slick parking lot toward the Toyota, so she kept moving, ignoring his urgent voice that came on a sudden gust of freezing air. "Wait, hear me out."

She was half inclined to stop, if for no other reason than it was the longest sentence the man had spoken all day. Maybe even since last night when she'd first laid eyes on him. But she'd had it with his strong-silent-type routine. Who was he? And what kind of game was he playing? A dangerous one? Her heart wrenched. It didn't make sense that the man had shown up in her life like this. *And why do his eyes look so much like Dylan's? Why does his body feel the same? How could I have been wrong?*

"And why's he here now? Following me?" she murmured, bitter air knifing into her chest as he pursued her. Once more, the words ran in her head like a mantra. *See her bleed. See her bleed.*

"Alice—"

"Get away!"

He didn't. At least she didn't think so. Not that she turned around. Another shudder moved through her, feeling doubly unsettling since it was from both fear and the cold. Who was this guy? And was there a reason why he'd appeared in her life when things were so precarious? Was it an accident? Coincidence? Thinking of Leland, she felt a slow icy stab jabbing at her heart. Well, she'd been right to break the engagement. The last hour in the sheriff's office proved that. So did the angry glimmer she'd seen in his eyes. She no longer even felt guilty about calling off the wedding. She only felt...

Terror. It curled through her veins as she recalled the almost predatory, possessive darkness in Leland's indigo eyes.

"Alice, I'm only asking you to stop for a minute."

Because she speeded her steps, going faster than the treacherously slick pavement really allowed, the rubber treads of her stylish fur-lined ankle boots lost traction. She gasped as she slipped, felt a muscle pull in her thigh, then she caught her balance and kept going. Twenty more feet and she'd be safe inside her car.

"Alice!"

At the urgency of his tone, she wrenched her head. The blustery wind blew back her hair, and she tried to ignore the tearing of her eyes and the sting of wind on her cheeks. Past Stuart Devlyn, she could see the yellow-brick building housing the sheriff's office, and she half wished she was back inside. Even facing Sheriff Sawyer and Leland was better than facing Stuart Devlyn.

Giving up and whirling fully around, she glared at him, fighting panic. "I'm warning you," she ventured. "Leave me alone." As if a mere female warning would stop a man like Stuart Devlyn.

But he did stop. Even from ten paces, she could see the watchful determination in his eyes. She glared back, fury vying with fear. Surely his being here wasn't unconnected to the other things happening in her life. She thought of the locket in her pocket again as her blazing eyes traversed the waning gray afternoon light. It was another bitter day, the kind where the air turned chalk-white and everybody's skin looked bloodless. A sudden blast shot through her wool coat with all the cold force of a bullet. She couldn't believe it. The jerk in front of her didn't even have God's good grace to be freezing. His thigh-length navy pea coat wasn't heavy enough for the weather, and yet he wore it open, the unbuttoned sides snapping like whips. He looked good, too, and she resented that—his wavy black hair blowing in the wind, flowing away from his chiseled face.

"Alice—"

Whatever it was, she wasn't about to listen. Turning once more, she strode the two remaining paces to her car and shoved the key into the lock. Just as she lifted the door handle, she felt him behind her. His breath was right near her ear and as warm as an oven; she spun around. Lord, was he close. "Stand back!"

His voice was low. "Not till we've talked."

Talked! Heat rushed into her cheeks. As if that was all the man—the stranger—had on his mind last night. "I don't have anything to say to you!"

"Judging from your tone—" He braced his ungloved hands on either side of her, pressing his palms against the car's frozen metal. "I think there's a lot you want to say to me right now."

Her heart ached. Was it her imagination, or had he really sounded a little like Dylan right then? "Get away from me!"

But he clearly wasn't going anywhere. Sudden, uncontrollable panic made her do what she'd never thought herself capable of. Raising her hand, she brought the flat of it good and hard against his cheek.

The smacking sound hung in the air.

His eyes narrowed; his lips compressed. She waited. For the first time, she was glad she wasn't wearing gloves. Nothing had ever felt quite so satisfying as slapping Stuart Devlyn. "I think," she announcing coolly, "*that* is all I have to say to you, Mr. Devlyn."

He hadn't so much as flinched, and the slap didn't seem to bother him any more than the cold. Sounding frustrated, he growled, "Oh yeah?"

It was a ridiculous thing to say, and the seeming hurt in his eyes acknowledged that. She said, "Yeah. And don't look so hurt. You're the one who *asked* what I think."

His eyes were even darker than usual, more black than brown in this light, or else they'd darkened with emotions she didn't want to contemplate. *Dylan's eyes.* She pushed away the thought. He said, "I know you're mad about—"

"Don't even say it!" she shouted, her fingers itching to slap him again. Before last night, she'd only given herself to one man—Dylan. Emotional pain caused her to suck in a breath. Yesterday seemed a million years ago. Had she really been about to get married again? She'd been trying to move on with her life. But now there were crank calls to contend with. Bloodred writing on the picture in the locket. Nancy Nolan's warning.

His voice was even. "Ready to talk?"

"No!" She moved to duck beneath his arm, hoping she could open the car door, get in and drive away, but his body was like an unforgiving wall of steel. "How many times do I have to tell you?" she gasped. "Let me go!"

"Sorry, but I can't. Not until we talk like two rational adults."

"Rational?" What happened last night was hardly rational. "I thought you were somebody else! And you knew it!" Her eyes bored into him. "No decent man would—"

His eyes said he hadn't been trying to be decent.

Her knees went weak as she remembered how easily he'd taken her over the edge, and her heart clutched. She loved Dylan, but last night this man... *I only responded like that because I've been alone so long.* And she'd liked it. As she tried to deny it, her eyes darted past him again, toward the sheriff's office. "I had reason to believe you were someone else," she repeated. "Someone...I loved..."

He raised an eyebrow. "Loved? But don't love anymore?"

"As if you have a right to ask."

He surveyed her, and when he spoke, she fought

the urge to shiver at the sound of his voice, which was gruff with seeming emotion. "Last night led me to think I could take certain liberties."

"Well, today you can't."

He stared at her. "Hmm. Well, I think I'll just take the liberty of asking one question, anyway. If you were so sure I was your husband, and if you were so in love with him, then why did you apparently annul your marriage to him? Why were you marrying another man?" Faint self-satisfaction twisted the corners of his lips. "Answer me that, Alice."

Before she could, he nodded as if to say, "I knew you wouldn't." Then his big strong hand swooped down and closed over hers. It left the impression of unforgivably smooth warmth right before he took away her car keys. She snatched the air, trying to get them back. "What do you think you're doing now? Taking my car?"

He met her gaze, his eyes unreadable, but she knew that's exactly what he intended to do.

There was no help for the righteous haughtiness that crept into her voice. "Really, Mr. Devlyn," she snapped. "I think you've taken enough already."

Anger flared in his eyes—and a challenge. "I didn't *take* anything," he corrected. "You gave." His gaze dropped a notch, and despite the frigid cold, and the strange circumstances, she became uncomfortably, unaccountably aware of her breasts beneath her coat. Damn. Why was she so powerless against her response to him? She thought of Dylan again and guilt flooded her. Glancing away, she reined in her emotions. Obviously Stuart Devlyn was a liar and a cheat, but her gut said he wasn't dangerous.

And he's right. I wanted him.

As she turned back to him, her cheeks warmed, flaming into a humiliated crimson that she'd give anything in the world for this man not to see. Lord, what was he thinking last night, when he'd lavished attention on her body, knowing she thought he was Dylan? "I bet you're getting off on this," she said coolly.

"Getting off on what?"

At least he had the good grace not to acknowledge the double entendre. "Humiliating me!"

"No," he said simply. "I'm not." And then he nudged her aside, opened the driver's door, nodded toward the passenger side and said, "I'm waiting."

She stared at him. "For what?"

"For you to get in."

"You can't drive my car!"

His brown eyes went unpredictably liquid again, as if she'd been privy to a sudden, quick view of the myriad angry emotions that seethed inside him, only to be cut off again. "C'mon, get in."

"For all I know, you don't even have a driver's licence. And if you do, you don't have it right now. The sheriff would have found it last night." She watched in stunned astonishment as he ignored the comment and slid past her and into the seat. As he turned the key in the ignition, he glanced up. "C'mon," he said again. And then he slammed the door.

Her eyes darted toward the sheriff's office. Not that anyone cared if this man stole her car. Her jaw set.

There was only one way to find out if Stuart Devlyn's appearance in her life had anything to do with the other strange things that were happening. Furiously circling the car, she got in. The second she shut the door, her heart thudded. Was she doing the right thing? Hazarding a quick glance at the man beside her, she suddenly decided she'd lost her mind. Why had she been so sure this was Dylan? And why had Nancy Nolan believed it?

"What's going on here?" she found herself saying as he pulled out of the parking lot and onto the road.

He cocked a thick dark eyebrow. "Going on?"

She heaved a sigh. "You know what I mean."

"Enlighten me."

"Not until *you* enlighten *me*."

Panic made her heart skip a beat as they zoomed along the main road; she could feel the locket through her coat and blazer pockets. Sweet memories of what this man had done to her last night in bed suddenly left her mind, leaving only terror.

And yet she was sure Stuart Devlyn was the key to everything that was happening to her. Which was why Alice, who was usually cautious and self-protective, had gotten into the blasted car with him. At least that's what she tried to tell herself.

But guilt flooded her when she glanced in his direction. Even now, she found herself noticing his good looks. With a sudden intake of breath, she glanced away from him, through the passenger window. The day seemed to look back at her—snowy-gray with dark barren trees. "Wait!" She suddenly gasped. He hadn't taken the turn to the ranch! "Where do you think you're going?"

"You'll see."

Her mind racing, she traced her eyes over the dashboard, then the gearshift. If she had to, could she quickly stretch her foot over the hump covering the transmission, grab the wheel and slam on the brake? Probably not. The roads were so icy that the car would spin if she tried to stop it. And he hadn't even asked her for directions, she realized. If he was really from L.A., how did he know where he was going?

Glancing over, he caught the panic in her eyes. "Don't worry."

She sent him a slack-jawed stare. "Telling me not to worry? That's supposed to make me feel safe?"

"You're fine," he assured her.

"Right," she managed to say as he drove into the mountains. And maybe she was. Somehow she believed this man. It was foolish, no doubt, but she did trust him. Sort of. At least enough that she was fighting the urge to open up and tell him what had been happening since yesterday. Absolutely no one on earth knew about the crank calls. Or about the locket. And the only reason she'd kept her mouth shut was to protect Dylan. But now she knew this man wasn't Dylan, and she was just as sure her hunch was right, that this man hadn't appeared by accident. He knew something. Maybe it was information that could help her find Dylan. *If Dylan's not dead.* Sudden tears stung her eyes. Yesterday, when she'd first seen the man who was now beside her, she'd felt such a rush of hope.

Realizing he'd pulled to the road's shoulder, she narrowed her eyes. "Why did you stop?"

He didn't answer, only looked past her and through her window, forcing her gaze to follow his. *Cat's Canyon.* She hadn't been here for years. Her breath caught, lodging in her throat. "Why did you bring me here?"

His eyes settled on hers. "You know why, Alice."

She did. But none of it made sense. All at once, she was sure this man and Dylan really were one and the same. And yet how could that be, when this man's fingerprints identified him as Stuart Devlyn, heir to the estate of a murdered musician? Fingerprints didn't lie. Her words were hoarse. "Why?"

"Because, Alice—" he leaned close, his voice going so soft it made her imagine liquid velvet "—it's where we first made love."

STUART DEVLYN, he thought. It was so strange to be called by a name he'd never heard. Stranger still to have a face so unlike his own. And to be told about the death of a father he'd never known he'd had.

He let the engine idle while his eyes took in the high, jagged, snow-covered mountain peaks blocking the already weak afternoon light. When his eyes returned to Alice's, he thought he'd never felt so conscious of her, of her soft scent, her shallow breaths. Her skin was the kind only true blondes possessed— winter-pale, flawless and so soft... The fabric of her camel coat looked soft, too. So touchable he longed to bury his face against the lapel. Her confused, lovely green eyes were brimming with questions, but she said nothing.

His voice came out low. "It's me, Alice. It's really me. I came back."

He didn't know what he expected, but more than the curt nod she offered. Impulsively, he reached for her, but she slipped from the embrace, crossed her arms and stared through the windshield. "Don't back away," he said, his voice catching. "I know I should have told you, but I couldn't..."

Her tone was sharp. "Couldn't?"

His voice dropped another notch until it was almost a whisper, laced with pain and begging for forgiveness because he'd left her. She had to understand he had no choice. "I couldn't tell you last night. I..." *Still feel I shouldn't, darlin'. I was going to leave.*

Seconds ticked by, and then she finally spared him a glance. "Your face?"

"I...had surgery. It was changed. It..." He could barely force himself to go into it. "Please don't be angry." He reached for Alice again, but she pulled away.

"Start talking."

He blew out a sigh, his heart aching. Was she really going to push him away? Keeping his emotions in check, he said, "I don't even know where to begin." *Or if I should at all.* "I...don't know how much I can safely say or not say."

Her voice was strangled. "You'd better tell me everything."

He didn't know what in her eyes urged him on more, the concern or smoldering betrayal, but something definitely made his heart do funny things; it pulled, ached and burned all at the same time. He could only imagine what this past twenty-four hours had done to Alice. Not to mention the past year and a half. Even so, a part of him—the better part—knew he should still walk away. "I don't want to hurt you, Alice. And if I talk to you now, I'll be putting you in danger."

Wary anger played in her eyes. "I'm already in danger."

Nothing could be further from the truth. He'd taken every possible precaution to protect her. He'd given practically everything but his very life to make sure she was safe. His eyes narrowed. "What do you mean?"

"I'm not saying until you tell me what's going on here." Her eyes wavered. "Dylan?"

He hated the telltale tremor in her voice as she spoke his name, as if she still wasn't entirely sure it was him. And what did she mean, she was in danger? Uttering a soft curse, he felt damned if he did, damned if he didn't. His heart hammered. "It's really me, Alice. I promise. And I haven't been trying to confuse you—"

"Maybe not, but you've been doing a good job of it."

"I'll tell you what I can."

"No!" she shouted. "You'll tell me everything! I thought you were dead!"

His lips parted in astonishment. "Dead?" He'd never considered that she might think such a thing.

"Dead," she emphasized.

He leaned closer, desperately wanting to hold her, but she scooted against the door. Her withdrawal made him that much more willing to talk and make her understand. "The day we got married," he began, "I was heading for the reception and someone attacked me in the church hallway..." He willed the memories by closing his eyes, and when he finally opened them, he told her the rest—how the attacker had thrown the plastic bag over his head, how the knife felt, wiggling against his throat.

Alice's tone held more than a trace of fear. "You were really attacked?"

"Yeah."

"Did you get a look at the person?"

"No. He was behind me the whole time." Fighting down a rush of shame, Dylan shook his head, still unable to believe he hadn't successfully defended himself. What kind of man let a knife-wielding maniac destroy his life?

Alice's voice shook, but he didn't know with what emotion now—fear or anger. "Whoever attacked you must have killed Jan."

He nodded. When Alice said nothing more, he stared through the windshield. Shadows were lengthening against the mountainous walls that formed Cat's Canyon, and as Dylan watched a hawk circle overhead looking for prey, he felt a sudden chill. Just like that hawk, someone was out there, stalking Dylan. And they had been since high school.

Alice was watching him guardedly. The disbelief and distrust in her eyes made him feel fresh hurt.

"Why didn't you find me?" she said. "Tell me? Tell the sheriff? You didn't even call. Where did you go?"

"Alice..." Dylan's voice trailed off, his lips parting in silent protest. Why couldn't she leave well enough alone? "Don't you trust me?"

She gaped at him. "Not anymore."

Didn't she understand he could never stop loving her? "Alice, I had to leave. He threatened to kill you. He said if I didn't walk away, walk right out of your life, that you'd die." Even now, the thought was more than Dylan could bear.

"And so you did? Just like that?"

He surveyed her. "Of course I did! What would you expect me to do?"

"Tell Sheriff Sawyer."

"And risk having you die?"

She nodded decisively, her cute, determined chin bobbing. "Yes."

He released a soft, exasperated breath. "I know what you must have gone through, Alice, but—"

"You have no idea!"

Suddenly it was too much. Even more overpowering than his desire to touch her. His voice turned gravelly, rough with emotion. "But I do. I know. I've gone through it, too, Alice. Every single day I've imagined what you're thinking. I've imagined your doubts. And I've shared your loneliness. Over and over, I've had to wonder if you thought I killed Jan. It never occurred to me that you might think I was dead. And when I found out you were marrying Leland..." Emotion ripped through him and he couldn't go on.

The soft catch in Alice's voice gave Dylan a glimmer of hope that she could still love him. "About Leland," she said. "It was…"

"Was?"

Alice offered a slight shrug. "We weren't in love."

Her eyes said the rest. She and Leland had been trying to be practical, to move on. And for that, Dylan felt only compassion. Lord, what had all their lives come to—his, hers, Leland's and Jan's? Dylan glanced around helplessly. Through the windshield, he watched the hawk's black silhouette trace another wide predatory circle in the sky. Suddenly the hawk swooped, diving straight down between the steep canyon walls, and Dylan found himself wondering what unsuspecting creature was about to die. Amazing, he thought, how much cruelty, uncertainty and danger there was in life. *And how much love.* Dylan hazarded a glance at Alice. *At least there used to be.* Clearing his throat, he continued, "I came back, Alice. But before I could, I had to do everything I could to disguise myself."

Her eyes flickered over him. "How? Who… operated? Where were you?"

He shrugged. "I, well, I did what the guy said at first. I walked right out of that church and never looked back." His voice rose. "And, Alice, I don't care what you think. Hate me if you want, but I'd do it again to keep you safe."

Darkness crossed her eyes, like storm clouds over a green lake, and only her trembling lower lip revealed the sweeter emotions she wanted to hide. "So why are you telling me this now? Why are you talking to me?''

"Because you were going to marry Leland. And I couldn't lose you. By the time I cleared my name— if I could—you'd have been married. I guess because I couldn't stand it anymore.''

Her voice was barely audible. "Where did you go?'' she asked again.

He shook his head grimly and exhaled another long sigh. "In my pockets, I only had the cash we were supposed to use for our honeymoon.'' Pausing, he tried to ignore the sudden, tight pull in his chest. He couldn't stand to think of their wedding day, a day so full of love and hope that had ended so badly. "I drove out of Rock Canyon,'' he managed to say. "I didn't get far. I wanted to think. I was considering coming back, but then Jan was murdered. I heard it on the news—I was staying in a cheap motel and...'' He glanced away. "When I heard they were looking for me as a suspect, I couldn't believe it. Me?'' His eyes searched hers. "What had I ever done to anybody? I worked hard, made good grades, played ball...'' He ran a hand raggedly through his dark hair. "And then I realized whoever attacked me and threatened you had killed Jan to make a point. He was letting me know that he was serious. He'd kill you, too.'' His heart ached as he thought of the friend he and Alice had lost.

"Or else he thought Jan was me.''

His heart clenched like a fist. He'd never even considered that. "What?''

"That's what people thought. It was an all-white wedding..." Her voice trailed off.

"I remember," he said softly. "Did you really think I could forget our wedding?" Reaching out a hand, he grazed a finger across the sleeve of her coat, but she edged away once more, discouraging contact, making his heart beat even faster. Didn't she know how badly he wanted to hold her right now? And she seemed to secretly want the same—at least judging from her eyes, which searched his new face, getting more accustomed to the changes. "Do you honestly think it was easy for me?" he finally asked. "Do you think I wanted to walk away?"

"I don't know."

He grabbed her hand. She let him hold it a second, then disengaged, pulling it from under his. The movement made his heart pull every which way. "Alice..."

She got back to business. "Jan was dressed like me. Our gowns weren't that different, our hairstyles were the same. And she was wearing my veil."

"Your veil?"

She nodded. "I'd put it on her head." The words cost her. He sighed sadly, remembering her and Jan, walking arm in arm, giggling together.

"It's not your fault," Dylan said softly.

Her eyes pierced his. "Whose is it, then?"

"I don't know. That's what I'm here to find out."

There was another slight tremor in her voice. "You were in the driveway. You didn't even come to my house. Were you even going to contact me?"

He wanted to lie, but couldn't. "No."

"Not even if I really married Leland."

"Then...yes."

"Couldn't you have called?"

He nodded. "I thought about it."

"But you didn't do it." She looked away. "Where did you go after the motel?"

"I ran." He sighed, telling her of all the places he'd been. "And then," he finished, "I wound up in Iowa. I found a plastic surgeon."

"Iowa?"

"I met him in a bar where I'd gone to look for work."

"You got a job?"

He nodded. "Yeah. I bartended a little. Anyway, the guy said he'd help me, so I gave him money I got from selling the truck. And then, he..."

"Made you look..."

Different.

And how. Dylan nodded grimly. Vaguely, he wondered what she thought of this new face. But the changes didn't matter. He was still the same man. Even last night, she'd known it was him.

Finally she said, "And then what happened?"

"And then somebody killed him."

She gaped. "Killed the plastic surgeon?"

He nodded. "I was about to leave town when he wound up dead. Stabbed in the alley behind the bar where I met him. I heard the cops said it was a routine mugging."

"But you don't believe it?"

He sat silently for a moment, then he shook his head. "I'm not sure. The doctor was an alcoholic, no doubt about it, judging from the way he was drinking when I met him in the bar. It was a low-class place, a real dive. And because he was rich and slumming it, it made sense that he'd get mugged. Still, as far-fetched as it was, I kept feeling that whoever killed him also killed Jan.''

"Why?''

He shrugged. "I really don't know. It was just a hunch. Maybe because of the way he was killed, with a knife. Or because of how the man in the church said he'd follow me. I don't know how he could have found me, but I'm sure he did. Maybe he was just sending another message, letting me know I was vulnerable. Maybe he wanted me to know he knew my face was different. Which meant if I came back here, you were still in danger.''

"Seems unlikely.''

"With you I couldn't risk it.'' His eyes lasered into hers and he wished like hell that he saw more warmth in her gaze. He ran his fingers through his hair, still feeling surprised at the touch. A body wave had left the strands feeling thick and coarse, but had served to further change his appearance. He sighed again. "This whole thing is unlikely, darlin'. Stranger than fiction. And then I got hit last night, and I didn't have a place to go...''

So I came home with you.

As if at the memory, unexpected temper crossed her features. "So, what's all this business about Stuart Devlyn?''

"I don't know.''

"You don't know?''

"No. That's the most disturbing thing. I've got no idea." His eyes sought hers. "I need to talk to Mom. I—I'm afraid that whoever attacked me also attacked her." He shook his head to clear it of confusion, his heart straining with the emotions of these past months. Including the new information that he was supposedly Stuart Devlyn. "Dammit," he said, "I don't know what's really going on. Who would have it out for me like this?"

"Someone does."

He shrugged. "I think of those calls I used to get back in high school. Remember?"

She nodded grimly.

He chewed his lower lip thoughtfully. "And I keep coming back to the idea that it's someone from school. Someone who's hated me ever since I moved to Rock Canyon. I just don't know who, though."

"I..."

His eyes locked on her face. "What? Do you know something?"

She looked undecided.

"Tell me."

"I...I was thinking about how competitive Leland used to feel toward you."

He nodded. He'd thought about Leland. "He was going to marry Jan, but he was always in love with you. And he wanted more responsibilities at the ranch..." Dylan paused. "While I was gone, I kept reading the local paper. And...I'm sorry about your dad." Her grateful eyes said she understood. Ward Eastman had been like a father to Dylan, and someday he hoped he and Alice would share more about their mutual grief. Now wasn't the time. "Leland," he continued. "I think he's jealous of me, but not a murderer. And now there's this."

"This?"

"Lang Devlyn." Dylan swallowed hard, wondering how much more to say. The dreams, or nightmares, that felt so much like memories were something he'd rather keep to himself. Mostly because he didn't understand their connection to his past. "Ever since I can remember, my mother and I were alone. We traveled around a lot until we got here and settled down. But she always told me my father was dead. And now, I guess she was married to Lang Devlyn. It seems incredible. Or maybe she wasn't married, which is why she didn't want to tell me about the relationship. Maybe she—"

"Your mother wouldn't live with a man without being married to him."

Alice had a point. A point he suddenly wished she was making while he held her tight in his arms. "No," he said. "I don't think she would. But then, why didn't she tell me who my father was? Or that he was still living?"

"I don't know." Color infused Alice's cheeks, making her look even more beautiful. "Last night…"

"Last night?" In the ensuing silence, his throat tightened, closing up, and disappointment filled him when she didn't reference their lovemaking, but said, "You seemed to recognize the estate on TV."

So she'd noticed. "I've seen it…in dreams. I couldn't believe it was right there, just as I'd imagined it. Alice, I didn't even know it was a real place until last night." He stared at her. "I really need to talk to my mother."

"*We* need to talk to her."

"We?"

He appreciated her desire to share their problems. He reached for her once more, instinctively closing his arms tightly around her and pulling her toward him in the seat. For the briefest second she let him press kisses to her cheek, and relief flooded him when he felt her soften against his chest. "I can't let you be involved," he murmured, brushing a hand over her silken hair. "I'm only telling you this because you're in so much pain from not knowing."

Abruptly, she backed away. "Gee, thanks," she muttered. "But what we once shared is over, Dylan. You could have relied on me—" Her voice broke. "The way a husband relies on a wife, but you chose not to."

"I know you're hurt," he murmured, barely able to stand how much the events of their recent past had hardened her.

"Hurt?" she echoed. Shoving her hand inside her coat, she dug into a pocket. "I'm not in pain."

He raised an eyebrow. "No?"

"No," she returned coolly. "I'm in danger." With that, she opened her fist, exposing the gold medallion she'd given him years ago. His lips parted in astonishment. And horror. Even now, he could feel it being wrenched from his neck. How the gold chain had cut into the flesh of his neck right before it broke.

His words were strangled. "Where did you get that?"

Just as he said the words, she flipped open the locket. Looking at it, he felt as if the floor had been swept from beneath him. He gasped. There—right over the lovely picture of Alice, written in tiny blood-red letters—were the words *See her bleed.* Dylan's heart pounded with fury. "Where did you get it?"

She looked at him long and hard. "From your bag."

He stared at her. "*My* bag?"

"From the bag the sheriff brought by this morning. The one you left at the Blue Sage Motel."

His heart pounded harder, now with fear. "Alice," he said. "You've got to believe me. I'd never seen that bag before."

Her eyes were wary. "The bag with your clothes?"

"Yeah. I've got no idea why the sheriff said it was mine."

"Because Clarisse, the woman who checked you into the motel, said she saw you with it."

"But she couldn't have."

Alice closed the locket and shoved it into her pocket again. "What do you mean, she couldn't have?"

He blew out a frustrated sigh. "She couldn't have because I never checked into that motel."

"But she saw you."

He shrugged helplessly. "If so, I have no recollection of checking in there." It made no sense. Was he going crazy? Sometimes his nightmares left him with such an odd feeling that he really did think he was going mad.

She said, "Then where were you staying?"

"Nowhere. I'd just gotten to Rock Canyon. I hitch-hiked in with a trucker." Suddenly, he grasped her hand. Even though she flinched, he held tight. "Don't you know what this does to me?" he said, sighing. "I don't know why the woman at the motel identified me. Maybe she was bribed. Don't you see? The bastard, whoever he is, can get to you, darlin'. This proves it. And so far, there hasn't been a damn thing I can do about it."

Pain threaded through her words. "Except leave me?"

"You were leaving me, too," he said softly. "You were marrying Leland."

Her eyes darted to his. "I had to move on. You were gone."

"Maybe I should have called," he said. "Or told you something. But I wanted to protect you." How could a man explain that to a woman? "I had to keep you safe. When a man can't do that..."

He's failed. As a man.

He blew out another sigh. "Right now, I don't even know who I am. Am I really related to Lang Devlyn? And who killed him? Is it possible it was the same person who attacked me in the church? The man who killed Jan? And why did my mother lie to me? Who's out to ruin my life?" There were so many questions that his mind was spinning.

"Whoever it is," Alice said, still keeping a phys-ical distance that was breaking his heart, "is also out to ruin mine. I've gotten crank calls. Warnings from your mother. And found this locket."

Before he could ask for more specifics, she said. "You left me and that's fine with me—"

"It's not fine. I didn't—"

"You did. And no man who loved me would have left. I don't want you back now. I—"

"Alice! I love you."

He couldn't believe the hurt in her eyes. "Doubtful."

The pain in that one word made clear that the past year and a half had taken far more of an emotional toll than he'd imagined. Before, she'd been so soft, gentle. And now he felt miserable. Still, he'd done the right thing. Regardless of what was to become of their personal relationship, he was going to continue protecting her. "I'm going to get the sheriff to guard you while I go to California."

"I'm the one who's in danger!" she shouted. "And because of that, even if you don't want me around, I'm going to be sitting right next to you on the plane."

"You're not going to California."

"Oh, but I am," she assured him. "And if you try to stop me, Dylan Nolan, I'll tell the sheriff everything, beginning with the murdered plastic surgeon in Iowa. I'll give Sheriff Sawyer all the proof he needs that you're Dylan Nolan. He'll haul you in and question you about Jan's murder." She nodded decisively. "And then I'll go to California by myself."

He didn't believe for an instant that she'd actually do that. "You've sure learned to fight dirty," he said.

"Just start the car," she returned.

He started to point out that the engine was already idling, but said, "The car?"

She nodded again. "Yes. We're going to talk to your mother at the hospital. And then we're going to California."

Chapter Ten

Fortunately, the Bel-Air Police Department wasn't inclined to alienate sons of murdered celebrities, and that was definitely working in Dylan and Alice's favor. Detective Louie Santiago was asking questions very gingerly. He was thin, slight of build, with smooth olive skin and slicked-back black hair. His starched white button-down shirt was tucked into navy slacks, and next to a red-white-and-blue tie, various pens stuck out from a pocket protector. "So you're telling me—" Santiago rolled an office chair closer to a gray lacquered desk as he scribbled on a legal pad "—that you never even knew you were related to Lang Devlyn?"

"That's right." Dylan nodded.

"Right," echoed Alice from the seat next to Dylan. She was wearing a red cotton cardigan over a silk sundress printed with sunflowers, and she looked as windblown as Dylan felt, with her sexily disheveled hair pinned back with clips. He glanced around. They had reservations at a nearby hotel—Alice had gotten them separate rooms—and their carry-on bags were beside the door. Alice had packed his, bringing some of his old jeans and shirts from his mother's cabin, and the fact that his mom hadn't given away the clothes—or the steel-toed boots he was wearing— made Dylan's heart ache with emotion. Lord, he could kill whoever had hurt his mother. He could still see her pale, unmoving body tucked beneath crisp white sheets in the River Run Hospital, and now, once more, he silently vowed to find whoever had beaten her to within an inch of her life.

He'd make Alice love him again, too.

Keep dreaming.

Glancing past her unforgiving profile, Dylan took in the Bel-Air Police Department, which was spacious and airy. The long, brightly lit hallways, open rooms of cubicles, new office furniture and plants made it seem more like an urban corporate headquarters than a place with jail cells. It was definitely a far cry from Sheriff Sawyer's office.

Dylan realized Santiago's eyebrow was raised. "Mr. Devlyn?"

Dylan glanced at Alice who was doing her best to keep her expression unreadable. He said, "Yes?"

Santiago was starting to look impatient. "You said you'd never heard Lang Devlyn was your father? Could you elaborate?"

Not much. Dylan considered, then said what he could. "I'd heard of Lang Devlyn. I mean, who hasn't? The man's a national figure. But..."

"But?"

Dylan shrugged and shook his head. "Never laid eyes on the man."

"And you thought your father was...?"

"Dead," Dylan said honestly. "Until I saw the fingerprint match in Sheriff Sawyer's office in Rock Canyon, and was told Lang Devlyn was my father."

"Speaking of Rock Canyon... Can you tell me what possessed you to go there?"

I went because I'm not just Stuart Devlyn. I'm also Dylan Nolan, and I wanted to see Alice and Mom, and to clear my name. Dylan's heart pulled. The past twenty-four hours had definitely further upset his world. Last night, the doctors hadn't let his mother talk much, but after the medical professionals had gone, when Dylan and Alice had been alone with her, he'd heard enough to know that Lang Devlyn really had been his father.

Who his mother thought *he* was, Dylan wasn't sure. She'd spoken only to Alice, and had regarded him with an unnerving mixture of fear and distrust. He'd tried not to take it personally, since coming out of a coma had to be disorienting. Regarding his father, Dylan knew the feelings hadn't truly touched him yet. He still felt numb, regretful that he'd never met Lang Devlyn, especially when he remembered his boyhood, and how much he'd wanted a father then.

But the father he'd never known was now dead. Murdered.

Dylan tried not to think of the grisly descriptions of how the father he'd never known had dragged himself from room to room, wallowing in his own blood. Vague, nebulous uneasiness uncoiled inside Dylan. He knew his mother well, and he loved her. But even more, he trusted her. Without just cause, she'd never have lied about his father being dead.

But now Dylan's father really *was* dead.

Was there a connection between his and his mother's flight from L.A. years ago, the events at the wedding, and Lang Devlyn's murder? And why had Dylan always been so haunted by visions of the lake at the Devlyn estate? It was far-fetched, but years ago, had his mother been fleeing from the same man who'd recently killed Lang Devlyn? Had that man killed Jan? Dylan sighed, wishing his mother was well enough to talk. As it was, she'd only offered Alice a few disjointed, rambling sentences.

Santiago said, "If you didn't know Lang Devlyn was your father, and if you had no contact with him, then who raised you?"

Dylan tried to look offended. Hell, what was he supposed to say? That he'd been raised in Rock Canyon, Wyoming, as Dylan Nolan? That Nancy Nolan was his mother? Hardly. If Santiago knew that, Dylan would be on the next plane back to Sheriff Sawyer—and probably wearing handcuffs. He'd be immediately arrested on suspicion of Jan Sawyer's murder. Dylan avoided Alice's eyes. "My life is very private." It was hardly a decent explanation for why he wouldn't talk, but it would have to do.

Santiago's gaze narrowed a fraction, but his voice remained light. "Right now, I can find no record of your life. No record of taxes." He paused. "Hmm. Well, I suppose your life will get private now that you're heir to an estate worth millions, huh?"

The air was squeezing from Dylan's chest, making

him feel vaguely panicked. "Is that an accusation, Detective? Do you think I've done something illegal?" Lord, was he going to wind up a suspect in yet another murder? First Jan and now this. Not to mention tax evasion....

In order to defend himself from such an accusation, he'd have to admit he was also Dylan Nolan. Yeah, it sure might seem as if he'd killed his father to get hold of an inheritance, too. Millions made for a strong motive. Especially since he and his father were estranged. "Am I under suspicion?"

Beside him, Alice sucked in an audible breath.

Somehow, the sound made Dylan recall the fear in her eyes when he'd driven up to Cat's Canyon. It was unsettling to realize she might have moments of doubt. Maybe she'd never love him again, but surely she didn't think him capable of murder. Or did she? Had she ever thought he'd killed Jan? And what did she make of the fact that there'd been a ticket from L.A. in the blue bag that was supposedly his?

Suddenly something seemed to crawl across Dylan's nape; the feeling was so intense that he lifted his hand and rubbed the spot. This whole situation was making his gut tighten into a knot. He knew damn well that the blue bag wasn't his. But whose was it? And why had Clarisse sworn he'd checked into the Blue Sage Motel carrying it?

She said she'd seen him. That was the most unsettling thing. Was it possible that Dylan was doing things of which he was unaware? *Had* he been in L.A.? *Had* he checked into the motel? Was it possible that he was having memory lapses? Blackouts of some kind?

Was it really possible to commit murder without knowing it? Could he have killed Jan Sawyer...?

Get a grip, Dylan. You didn't kill anyone!

Feeling uneasy, Dylan shifted in his chair as if to ground himself, then he stared at Santiago, who was still considering, now gazing down at his legal pad and worrying his lip between a thumb and index finger. Hell, maybe the detective meant for this long silence to unnerve Dylan and Alice. If so, Dylan decided, his tactics were working.

Finally, Santiago said, "No. You're not under suspicion, Mr. Devlyn. But that plane ticket in your bag does place you in L.A. at the time of the murder. Look, I can't make you answer any of my questions, not unless I'm charging you, which I'm not. So far, there's nothing at the scene of the crime—at your father's house," he amended, "that indicates you were on the premises. I haven't Mirandized you, and since you don't know me from Adam, you know you don't owe me a thing. But still, uh, let's just say your hesitation is more than a little unusual." The sensible plea in Santiago's dark eyes was nearly irresistible. Dylan guessed he was a good cop. "C'mon," Santiago finished, "what do you have to lose by helping me out here? If I can't get information voluntarily, I will have to resort to other means."

Dylan's eyes slid to Alice's hands, which were resting on her knees. What he wouldn't give right now to thread his fingers through hers and squeeze, and to feel her squeeze back.

Santiago sighed. "Okay. Have it your way. Mind taking a look at this?"

Dylan's heart skipped a beat as the detective slid a faxed page from a Rock Canyon High School yearbook across the desk. "As you both know, the Rock Canyon sheriff is still looking for this man." Santiago glanced at Alice. "I believe he was your husband?"

Alice's features remained masked. "Yes. Uh, the marriage was annulled."

Dylan's chest constricted. Under the circumstances, he didn't blame her for that. Probably her parents had pressured her to annul the marriage. But it still hurt. Dammit, Alice was supposed to be his. *Until death us do part.*

"That's a picture of Dylan Nolan," she clarified.

Santiago nodded. "And he's still at large."

Alice's eyes slid to Dylan's again. She cleared her throat. "I...don't know. I—I always thought Sheriff Sawyer should have investigated further, that something might have happened to Dylan."

Santiago stared deeply into her eyes. "Something?"

Alice nodded. "Something bad. That he could have been murdered, the way Jan Sawyer was."

Dylan decided it was bad enough to be sitting here under the circumstances, but did Alice really need to elaborate on their marriage? Or his disappearance? Still, she was throwing Santiago off the scent, which was good. After all, the detective kept glancing curiously between Dylan and Alice as if he knew there was more to the relationship than met the eye. Dylan bit back a sigh. He only wished there was more to it.

But maybe the events in their lives had driven an irreparable wedge between them. Alice seemed intent on rejecting him.

Santiago said, "Uh, Mr. Devlyn, do you know Dylan Nolan?"

Dylan tried to look casual, but staring down at the picture did strange things to his insides. Hard to believe the boy with the fleshy, cherubic cheeks and golden windblown hair was him, and that Santiago didn't realize it. Somehow, Dylan expected the man to see similarities, maybe to recognize the eyes. But even Dylan himself was shocked when he looked into mirrors now and saw a stranger staring back. No, the boy in the picture didn't resemble the dark-haired man with the chiseled face whom Dylan had become.

"Recognize him?" Santiago prodded.

Dylan could barely believe he was being asked to identify himself. His voice was deceptively even. "No. Any reason I should?"

Santiago paused a long moment, his dark eyes assessing Dylan's. "We think…he might be your brother."

"What?" Dylan felt as if the wind had been knocked out of him. Beside him, Alice looked equally stunned. Now Santiago was convinced that Dylan was his own brother! This was so ludicrous. "As far as I know, I don't have a brother." But then, he hadn't known he'd had a living father, either.

"*A brother?*" Alice now echoed.

Santiago nodded. "A woman in the hospital in Rock Canyon, a woman who's been living there for years and going by the name Nancy Nolan is really

Lang Devlyn's estranged wife.'' Santiago nodded at Alice. "I'm talking about your ex-mother-in-law. As you know, she worked on your family's ranch. Now, as near as we can tell, she fled Los Angeles a little over twenty years ago, though we don't know why. And she took one of her and Lang Devlyn's sons.''

One of them?

Dylan kept his expression unreadable, but his mind was spinning. What was going on here? Would he ever be able to untangle this web of lies?

"Mr. Devlyn?" prompted Santiago.

"Sorry," Dylan managed to say. "But this is all so painful to listen to." Suddenly he wished he could tell Santiago that he was Dylan Nolan and that Nancy was his mother. Maybe Santiago could help. But more likely, Dylan would wind up in jail, being charged with Jan Sawyer's murder. And then Alice might further endanger herself by deciding to play sleuth on her own.

Not that Dylan blamed her. Every strange thing that had happened was connected: Jan and Lang Devlyn's murders, the attack on Dylan's mother, the phone calls Alice had gotten and the defiled picture in her locket.

Dylan could feel it in his gut. So could Alice. It was why she'd been hell-bent on accompanying him here. Otherwise, she was hardly speaking to him. He'd been watching her profile as they landed in L.A., and he'd seen something so uncompromisingly regal in it that he still hadn't shaken the bone-deep hurt. Why couldn't she accept that he'd left for her own good?

"I'm very sorry to have to ask these questions," Santiago was saying now.

"It's all right," Dylan said.

In the next long silence, Dylan glanced through a window. From the ground, L.A. looked beautiful. Bright sunlight filtered through the fronds of palm trees and countless sprinklers were trained on blooming flowers and lush green grass. From the air, it was another story. Looking past Alice's profile as the plane landed, Dylan had been staring into a layer of brown haze. Haunted skyscrapers were shrouded in brown mist. They'd looked like his own life felt— hidden and mysterious. On the ride from the airport to the hotel, Dylan hadn't been able to keep his eyes from the oleander that was planted along the freeways, to keep wild animals from running onto the roads. Just looking at the plants made Dylan shudder.

He realized Santiago was still surveying him, looking cautious and puzzled. "All we have that identifies you—and it's plenty—are your fingerprints. Your father put them on file with us years ago, in case you were ever kidnapped." He shrugged. "As Sheriff Sawyer probably told you, it's pretty common around here."

"Lots of rich, famous people in the neighborhood, huh?" said Alice, sounding vaguely relieved that Santiago had introduced a new topic.

"Bel-Air's definitely got its share."

"I can't imagine living that way," Alice said, a soft twinge in her voice. "I mean, fearing a ransom call. I guess a lot of celebrities have to worry about that."

Santiago shrugged again. "Yeah. Anyway, it seems that Dylan Nolan was also the son of Lang Devlyn. At least that's my guess, since Nancy Nolan was married to Lang, and they did have two sons." He nodded at Dylan. "Stuart Devlyn. And Niles Devlyn. Of course, we've got no way to find out if the boy who Nancy raised as Dylan Nolan is really Niles Devlyn. We can hardly check Dylan Nolan's prints against the ones Lang left in our file, since..."

"Since Dylan vanished?" Alice finished.

Santiago nodded. "Sheriff Sawyer had Dylan Nolan's prints on file, but they moved offices a while back, and have misplaced the files. Apparently, Dylan was fingerprinted after a boyhood prank, but the files weren't stored with those of more serious crimes. Sheriff Sawyer's still looking for the files."

Dylan's gut clenched. It was bad enough that Sawyer might soon find his fingerprints. But in addition to the father he'd never known, did Dylan also have a brother? He could still barely register the information. "Lang Devlyn definitely had two sons?"

Santiago nodded. "Yes."

"You're sure?" prodded Alice.

"Sure am."

There was a long pause. Santiago tried again. "Uh, you're being truthful when you say you have had no ties to your father, is that right, Mr. Devlyn? You really didn't know he was your father?"

Dylan sighed. He supposed the detective was trying to wear him down. "I've told you the truth."

"So who was your mother? Who raised you?"

Dylan said the only thing he could. "I've answered enough for now."

Alice sounded offended. "Like he said, he's a very private man."

Santiago's eyes zeroed in on Alice. "What possessed you to travel here with a stranger you only met the night before last? Mind telling me that?" When she didn't answer, Santiago shifted his gaze to Dylan and continued, "As I said, we know your father was once married to Nancy Paul aka Nancy Nolan. Paul was her maiden name. Anyway, we've now established that she's been living in Rock Canyon, which is where we found you yesterday. She raised a son there who vanished after a murder that occurred on his wedding day..."

Whatever Santiago was digging for, Alice wasn't about to let him have it. "Maybe when Ms. Nolan is well, you'll get some of your answers, Detective."

"I'm sure I will," murmured Santiago, suddenly sounding absent. For a long moment, he stared down at his pad again, then he abruptly glanced up, his eyes searching Dylan's. "I really need to know more about you—where you grew up, who raised you, what you were doing in Rock Canyon." His lips pursed. "And I will get the information. Right now, I'm just trying to make things easy for you."

Dylan really didn't know what to say. He knew he sounded like a broken record. "My life is very private."

"You said." Santiago tapped a pencil against the legal pad. "And as of today, you're a rich powerful man in Los Angeles, too, which means I don't want to step on your toes.''

There was a touch of awe in Alice's voice. ''Rich?'' she murmured, her voice barely audible. ''It's hard to believe.''

Santiago nodded thoughtfully. ''The information I asked Sheriff Sawyer to convey is correct. Stuart's inherited the bulk of the Devlyn estate. In fact, there's a lawyer—'' Pausing, Santiago scribbled on a corner of the legal pad, ripped off the paper and pushed it at Dylan. ''His name's Ben Rose. He wants to meet you at the estate when we're done here, which I guess we are.'' Santiago didn't look too happy about the small amount of information he'd received, but he wasn't the type to waste his time. He turned to Alice again. ''It really was so nice of you to come here with Mr. Devlyn.''

She smiled coolly. ''I do pride myself on being a nice person.''

Everything in Santiago's eyes said he knew there was more to her motives than met the eye. ''Do you?''

''Yes, Mr. Santiago.''

''Then maybe you'd like to stay just one more minute, and tell me whatever you can about the woman you knew as Nancy Nolan. The sheriff tells me that you married her son...'' *And that he vanished after your wedding, the day of Jan Sawyer's murder.*

The unspoken words hung in the air. ''We never knew anything about her background,'' Alice said calmly. ''I can tell you that much. When she took the job at the ranch, working for my father, she told him she'd had other kinds of work experience. Waitressing, clerking in a clothing store.''

"She didn't seem out of place in Rock Canyon?''

Alice suddenly stared down. Fidgeting a moment, she finally folded her hands in her lap. Dylan didn't know, but he thought she might be remembering that day, years ago, when they'd met outside the general store. "Nancy Nolan did seem a little out of place in Rock Canyon,'' Alice continued. "She was glamorous somehow. But we never would have guessed she'd been a singer out here in L.A.''

Nor could Dylan. His eyes strayed to an album cover on Santiago's desk. The detective had told them that, apparently, in 1969, when his mother was only seventeen years old, she'd been a backup singer with a little-known group called the Micro-Velvets. By then, Lang Devlyn had already faded into relative obscurity. His own singing career was over, and it was while he was scoring movies and producing records that he met, and married, Nancy Paul. He'd backed the two albums the band had produced. But what happened to the couple after that was still up for conjecture.

"Is there any evidence that my father was abusive to...'' My mother? "To Nancy Paul Devlyn?'' Dylan asked.

Santiago shook his head. "No.'' He shrugged. "The marriage dissolved a long time ago, but we're doing our best to interview people connected to Nancy and...'' Santiago paused. "Your father.''

Father. Even now, it sounded so strange to Dylan. Santiago lifted eyes that were deceptively patient.

Come hook, crook or nail, Santiago was going to get his answers. Oh, for now, he'd let Dylan and Alice walk away, but he'd solve his case. And he'd find out where Dylan—aka Stuart Devlyn—had spent the last years of his life.

"Your mother and father had a very private relationship," Santiago said thoughtfully, "far outside the public eye. It wasn't even really public knowledge that your father married. In fact, he may well have had other secret marriages for all we know. Sometimes stars are married outside the country, and don't have U.S. records. Near as I can tell, so much money was, and is, being made off the Lang Devlyn image—" Santiago paused and shrugged, as if he'd suddenly grown bone-weary of Los Angeles celebrity types. "He was the quintessential lone-man, a rebel without a cause. And re-releases of his old records on CD are still selling briskly. So, from a marketing standpoint, keeping private affairs out of the limelight was key. After he and Nancy were married, they seem to have cut off other relationships. Nancy quit singing with the Micro-Velvets...."

Dylan didn't say anything.

For the first time, Santiago looked genuinely frustrated. "Christ, c'mon," he suddenly muttered. "I've been trying to follow every lead possible in solving your father's murder. If you won't tell me everything you can, how can I find out if someone from the past might want him dead? How can I—"

Santiago suddenly quit rambling. His eyes seemed to shift, to become more sharply focused. "Sheriff Sawyer found the ticket from L.A. in your bag, Stuart.

So please. One more time. We'd like to know what you were doing in L.A.''

Stuart. Hearing the name spoken out loud was jarring.

Dylan hazarded a quick glance at Alice—and his heart ached, the way it did every time he looked at her. She was seated next to him, so close that he'd barely need to move his hand to hold hers. Perched on the edge of her chair, she looked heartbreakingly willing to help, even though she'd made clear their personal relationship was over.

Or at least on hold.

On hold. Dylan had to think that's all it was. Her eyes caught his. She understood his dilemma, but had no idea what he should say to Santiago. He finally settled on the truth.

"I truly have no recollection of being in L.A."

Santiago raised an eyebrow. "What?"

"You heard me."

Santiago squinted. "But what about the ticket that was found with your belongings?"

"I…" Dylan glanced at Alice again. If only she knew how much strength and comfort he was drawing from her presence. "I'd never seen that bag."

"Never?" Santiago clarified.

Dylan shook his head. "I had a bag. An army duffel. But the trucker I hitched into Rock Canyon with drove off with it." Dylan shrugged. "I'd thrown it behind the front seat, and when we reached Rock Canyon, we planned to part ways. At the gas station in town, I hopped out to go to the john, meaning to come back for the duffel. But when I got there, the guy had already driven off. Apparently he thought I'd already taken my gear.''

Santiago's eyes sparked with interest. ''What did he look like? What kind of truck?''

Dylan thought back. ''The truck had a red Peterbilt cab, and the guy said he was hauling canned goods. He was a big guy. Heavy with black hair and a beard. He looked kind of like Jerry Garcia.''

Santiago squinted. ''From the Grateful Dead?''

''The Grateful Dead?'' echoed Alice.

Dylan nodded. ''The band,'' he clarified.

''Oh,'' Alice said. ''Right.''

Under other circumstances, Dylan might have smiled. Alice wouldn't recognize the name immediately because her taste ran to country music. Suddenly, he was remembering other little things about her. How she hated her hair in her eyes, which was why she clipped it back. How her favorite smells were saddle leather and lilacs.

''The man had Michigan plates,'' Dylan continued, ''and he said his wife's name was Ursula.''

Santiago quit scribbling. ''We'll find him.'' He narrowed his eyes. ''But if what you're saying is true, then how do you account for the fact that you were identified as carrying that bag into a motel in Rock Canyon?''

Dylan spoke honestly. ''I can't.''

Santiago's lips pursed. ''If you don't, I'll probably be arresting you by tomorrow.''

''I didn't kill my father.''

''No, it doesn't look that way. There's no evidence.

But the lack of tax records… Well, I can't make you tell me more, I guess.''

"There's nothing to tell.''

"At least tell me what you were doing in Rock Canyon.''

Dylan managed a shrug. "Just taking a vacation.''

Santiago's assessing eyes shifted curiously between Alice and Dylan. Santiago seemingly sensed everything—that Stuart was really Dylan Nolan, and that he and Alice had been married. It wouldn't even take a detective, Dylan decided, to feel the world of tension that lay between him and Alice.

Santiago frowned. "Unfortunately the man who handles the estate's security is out of town. While we've watched tapes from the cameras we've found, the estate is large and the security system elaborate. We're hoping we'll find more hidden cameras and tapes that might show us something.'' He glanced between Dylan and Alice again. "Meantime, I guess you'll want to head out to the estate. Like I said, Ben Rose is waiting. We've let him get some of your father's private papers. And he wants to talk to you.''

Dylan said, "About?''

"The will, Mr. Devlyn.'' Santiago's eyes suddenly looked thoroughly unkind. "When it comes to that,'' he said, "I'm sure you'll be willing to talk.''

What the man really meant, Dylan knew, was that the millions he'd just inherited was a good motive for murder.

Chapter Eleven

Alice was watching him carefully. "Do you remember this place? You said when you were watching TV, you did."

Dylan nodded. His voice was low. "Like I said, I thought it was from a dream." *Or a nightmare.* "I wasn't sure it was real."

Alice sighed grimly. "It doesn't get any more real than this."

"That's for sure."

Cops were everywhere. Dylan and Alice had been directed down a long red-carpeted hallway toward Lang Devlyn's office, but they'd paused in front of a window overlooking the lake. Outside, the landscaped grounds seemed innocuous enough—if not for the uniformed officers and plainclothes detectives, the yards of yellow cordoning tape. Inside, blood was still visible on the black-and-white marble floor of the foyer. Just seconds ago, a policeman had nodded toward the floor, then pressed a business card into Dylan's hand.

"You'll need a cleaning service," he'd said. "This

one specializes in crime scenes. Another twenty-four hours and you can call.''

Dylan guessed he'd have to. After all, this estate with its vast acreage, mansion and memories was now his. *Innocuous,* he thought now, his eyes roving over the scene. *Hardly.* The window, only inches from his eyes, was so squeaky-clean that the glass seemed nonexistent, and through it, he took in the dense thickets of trees and far-off stone wall, the interior side of which was planted with oleander. Closer, a light California breeze washed over the lake's dark surface, rearranging sunlight on the water, causing shimmers and ripples. His eyes settled on the swing set facing the lake; propelled by the breeze, two swings dangled, swaying.

Suddenly, Dylan imagined the breeze against his cheeks. He was swinging again, staring down at the grass, then flying high into the air.

You get everything.

Do not.

Do, too.

He remembered the words, probably heard years ago. Was the speaker the brother he'd never known he'd had? And if so, where was that brother now? Why had Dylan's mother fled Lang Devlyn's house— *this* house—and left her other child behind? What kind of mother would do that? *She wouldn't,* Dylan thought. *No matter what, my mother would never do that.*

"C'mon." Alice's voice gentled. "We'd better get back there. Ben Rose is waiting."

Dylan nodded, but he still didn't move. "I feel that if I just stand here long enough, I'll remember..."

What?

He didn't even know. All he knew was that he could feel Alice's vital warmth a half foot away, and that warmth was keeping the prickly chill at his neck from crawling down his spine. He felt her move closer, and surprisingly, her hand, small and soft and smooth, slipped into his. Grateful, he curled his fingers around hers. After another second, hers tightened, making him wonder if she had any inkling how much he needed her right now. He wished she didn't know his true identity because she'd be safer that way, but her quiet, female strength was keeping him anchored.

Gentle jolts of awareness coursed up his arm from the touch of her fingertips. His voice was gravelly. "Thanks, Al." *Al.* It was the first time he'd called her that in a long time.

As if she'd suddenly remembered her anger at him, her softly spoken words carried a trace of stiffness he wished would vanish. She said, "For?"

"For just being here."

As if realizing she'd come a fraction too close, she let her hand slip from his again, but he didn't mind. She'd reached out. That alone told him she hadn't really closed the door on their relationship. She cared for him; she'd never stopped. There was hope she'd forgive him for leaving. He knew she would if she truly understood the danger they were in.

"C'mon," she said again.

Turning from the window, he glimpsed the foyer's

marble floor and his gaze trailed where blood smeared across the black-and-white marble squares. There was something strangely unreal about the red swaths. The big washy strokes could have been painted by a life-size paintbrush. Lord—Dylan suddenly felt vaguely queasy—was that really blood?

My father's blood.

With a quick shudder, he turned away. "Well," he said, as he and Alice began walking down the hallway again, "I guess we'd better see what Ben Rose has to say."

AT FIRST IT WASN'T MUCH, just a rambling list of Lang Devlyn's considerable assets, to which Dylan and Alice listened uncomfortably from two over-stuffed chairs while Ben Rose talked. The man was in his sixties, nattily dressed in a linen suit that was the same snowy white as his full head of bushy hair. While he explained things, he brushed back his hair with a harried hand and rested his considerable bulk against the corner of a dark-wood desk that had elaborately clawed feet.

Dylan tried to listen, but his mind strayed. Everything in the room tugged at him—from the heavy brocade curtains, to the chandelier, to the shelves of collector's books about movies and music. Each item was jogging elusive memories that always remained just out of reach. Besides that, the place was too opulent for Dylan's comfort.

His eyes met Alice's. She, too, was accustomed to simpler, more rustic surroundings. While the main house at the Eastman ranch was large, it was homey, with a big, airy kitchen, ruffled curtains and the sweet scents of baking. Chairs tended to be well cushioned but more functional than the brocade seats Dylan and Alice now occupied, and the ranch's front entry, while clean, was apt to be strewn with riding gear— saddles and bridles, dusty gloves and mud-caked boots.

A far cry from this place. Dylan glanced toward the foyer of the Devlyn estate again. With a glance, Alice said she shared his thoughts.

"Mr. Devlyn, will you be moving these accounts?"

"We'll leave them as they are for the time being," Dylan said. *At least until I figure out what's going on here.*

"Well, if you decide you want any cash transferred…"

Dylan didn't hear the rest. His gut had clenched again, balling up like a fist as his eyes settled on a letter opener. It was on the desk, just inches from Ben Rose's blousy white pant leg. Staring at it, Dylan suddenly remembered running through this very room, his footsteps pounding.

"Stop or I'll kill you."

Was that his brother's voice? Someone else's? Dylan didn't know, only that he'd whirled toward it, his heart jabbering frantically just as the letter opener came down in a silver flashing arc.

"I'm gonna tell," Dylan had cried.

"Crybaby, crybaby," came the mocking voice. *"I'm gonna tell."*

Shutting his eyes, Dylan wondered how old he'd

been, but no matter how hard he tried, he couldn't remember. Still, when he opened his eyes, he found himself remembering other things. Or maybe not really remembering…just *knowing*. He knew where the kitchen was in this house, for instance, and that cookies used to be kept in the bread box. He knew that the clothes closets were cedar-lined, and that at Christmastime, he would sing, reading the words to carols from a book while someone played the piano. His father maybe?

Read?

Lord, had he been able to read when he'd lived in this house? *Lived*, he thought. Yes, now he was sure he had lived here. Exactly how old had he been when his mother fled? What memories had he repressed? Blocked out? If he could read, he'd have to have been at least five or six when he left…

Stop or I'll kill you.

He could still hear that voice. Had someone really been trying to kill him? Is that why he couldn't remember more? A shot of adrenaline went through him, and he was still fighting the urge to get up and pace the room when something in Ben Rose's voice brought him back to the present. The lawyer was now speaking in hushed tones, almost conspiratorially, and his piercing blue eyes were scrutinizing the study's empty doorway, as if he were making sure no police officers were listening. "The police are asking me and your father's accountant about these financial dealings," he was saying. "They've noticed that large amounts of cash have been siphoned off. But because your father's a public figure, and because he wanted matters concerning your brother kept private, we haven't answered any questions yet. The large sums used for your brother will need to be explained to the police...somehow. But we need to know from you, uh, what exactly you want to say. How you want us to proceed.''

Realizing his eyes had settled on Alice's, Dylan tore them away. "You know my brother?''

There was a long pause. "No. Of course not. Not really. In fact, I've only recently traced where he is. Arrangements for his care have always been handled by a third party, in the interest of keeping the whole affair quiet.'' There was another uncomfortable pause. "As you can understand, Stuart, your father never wanted the public to know he existed. Which is why records have been kept untraceable.''

Dylan's heart hammered. What was wrong with his brother? Why had he been hidden away? His concern was mirrored in Alice's gaze.

"Please go on, Mr. Rose,'' she prompted.

Ben's eyes settled kindly on Dylan's. "I know this must be difficult for you, and I very much doubt you'd want to see him. But he's currently in a place called the Highland Home.'' Reaching, Ben fished through a file. "The address is right here. The place isn't far away. You'll find it in the Hollywood Hills.'' Handing the address to Dylan, Ben continued, "In case you want to check it out yourself. The facility's exclusive and expensive. I mean, absolute top dollar. It's really up to you whether or not to continue with the same level of care. You might want to find some-thing less costly.''

Dylan was staring blankly down at the paper. "The Highland Home," he murmured.

Alice cleared her throat awkwardly. "Mr. Rose," she said, "would you mind telling us why he's there?"

During another long pause, Dylan glanced up, into Ben Rose's quizzical eyes. "Yes," Dylan echoed. "Why?"

"Surely," Ben returned slowly after a stunned moment, "while only myself and two other of your father's associates were ever told of this, you—of all people—must know."

Dylan's chest felt tight. "Know what?"

Ben Rose looked vaguely stupefied. "That your brother was committed after trying to kill you."

"YOU SAY you're *Stuart Devlyn?*" The head psychiatrist and director of the Highland Home, Dr. Clark, froze in misstep. For a long moment, his fearful owlish brown eyes flitted around a ground-floor room that, because of its antiques, fireplace and tastefully framed line drawings, looked more like a sitting room in a private residence than an office. "But you...you can't be."

"He is." Alice stepped forward and grasped the man's dangling hand, shaking it.

The contact seemed to bring Dr. Clark back to his senses. He blinked, then he ran a flat palm down the front of a chocolate brown double-breasted suit jacket, as if making sure he was presentable. He was thin, wiry and bookish, with a high forehead and receding hairline that made him look smarter than average.

"Stuart Devlyn?" he repeated. "Really?"

Dylan fished a copy of the facsimile that identified his fingerprints from a jeans pocket. "I realize not many people know about my brother's confinement, Dr. Clark," he said. "But you can talk to me. I really am Stuart Devlyn."

"Please," Dr. Clark said shakily, "take a seat."

The psychiatrist seated himself in an armchair, held the paper between trembling fingers and perused it, while Dylan sat down next to Alice on a silk-upholstered settee. Glancing over, he could tell she was as excited as he; her skin was flushed, and the pulse beat was visible in her pale neck. On the way over in the rental car, she'd talked nonstop, just the way she used to, which touched his heart. Not that she'd let him get any physically closer to her, though he'd tried.

Now Dylan just wished all her questions weren't so grim. Unfortunately, Ben Rose had been unable to tell them more about Niles Devlyn, although Ben did confirm that Nancy Devlyn had fled the Devlyn estate twenty-one years ago.

"She raised you under another name?" the lawyer had asked.

"Yes." Dylan had conceded that much, since Ben clearly wasn't going to talk to the police before Dylan had a chance to speak with Dr. Clark about his brother.

"Your father had P.I.'s looking for you for years," Ben had also said, and the information nearly did Dylan in. Had his father really missed him? Wanted to know him? Dammit, why had his mother run away and deprived him of a father?

Oh, c'mon, he thought now. *You remember, don't you, Dylan?*

Now, sitting in Dr. Clark's office, he felt suddenly breathless. He could feel the panic coming back, the sense of suffocation, the fear as cold water seeped through his clothes. Twisting, he tried to get free of the hand that held him in the murky depths of the lake. Lungs burning, he kicked at the water. Muffled splashes sounded.

And then everything went black...

Dylan drew a deep breath. Coming back to the present, he felt his eyes follow Alice's, which had skated toward a window. The Highland Home was definitely pricey. Wrought-iron gates linked stone walls that surrounded extensive, well-tended grounds. Fancy lawn furniture was artfully arranged around a well-stocked goldfish pond. Farther away were badminton nets, tennis courts and a pool.

The place could have been a resort for the rich and famous. But something gnawed at Dylan—maybe at anyone who visited—and after closer inspection, other things became apparent: close-circuit televisions, cameras in the trees, cleverly concealed mesh over the windows, that there were bars inside some of the vehicles. Faint, unsavory smells glided along the baseboards, too, as if something frightening lurked under the floor. Yes, closer inspection reminded visitors that this was a resort—but only for the dangerously insane. Alice's gaze returned to Dylan's and they exchanged a worried glance.

"Remarkable," Dr. Clark murmured, still staring at the facsimile.

"Yes?" Dylan prompted.

Dr. Clark gazed into his eyes. "Well, your face, Mr. Devlyn, I just wasn't expecting..."

Dylan's heart skipped a beat. What could this man possibly know about the changes in his appearance? "My face?"

Dr. Clark's voice lowered, catching with anguish. "I don't blame you for changing it, Mr. Devlyn. It was the smart thing to do."

"Smart?" He was beginning to feel like a parrot, but he didn't know what else to say.

The director gave an uncharacteristic shudder. "I've worked with the insane for years. But to be perfectly honest, your twin brother unsettled me. He hated you so much."

Twin? Dylan's mind raced. That would explain so much. Why, in his dreams, Dylan had so often turned to see another boy who looked like him. He'd be swinging, and yet turn and see himself swinging.

Or see myself drowning myself.

Or see myself trying to stab myself with a letter opener.

"Did he?" Dylan managed to say. "Hate me?" With the words, he felt that cold clammy hand again, wrapping around his neck. Swallowing hard, he stared at the director, sizing him up. Dr. Clark peered back as if he'd long wanted to unburden himself. But what did the man want to be free of?

Dylan exchanged another glance with Alice. Everything in her eyes indicated she was reading his thoughts and fears. That alone took his breath. Didn't Alice understand how important that was? How unusual? People could search a lifetime and never find someone with whom they could communicate without words.

Her eyes were urging him on. "Tell him..."

"Okay," Dylan murmured, knowing what she was thinking. He took a deep breath. And painstakingly at first, then with words that flowed, he told the director everything he could, leaving out only one crucial fact, that Stuart Devlyn was also known as Dylan Nolan. Otherwise Dylan detailed the events of the past forty-eight hours and honestly expressed that he could remember little of the past, nor recall much about his father or brother.

"I don't know if you can help us, Dr. Clark," Dylan finished, "but I hope you'll try. As the head of a psychiatric facility, I'm sure you realize that my memory losses are..." He finally settled on, "Worrisome."

"I imagine *terrifying* might be closer to the truth," Dr. Clark offered gently.

Dylan nodded, his chest pulling with the full realization that recovering his memory could cure him of the feelings of dislocation he'd suffered for years. "Given what I've heard, I think I want to meet my brother."

Maybe it was the wrong thing to do, but Dylan was curious. And surely seeing Niles face-to-face would jog more memories.

"Dear Lord." Dr. Clark rose abruptly and crossed to the window. "I hope you never do meet him. If you want to, you'd be as mad as he." Pausing, he stared out at the grounds a long time. Automatic sprinklers that were trained on the flower beds came on.

"What can you tell us about him?" Alice said, her voice anxious.

Dr. Clark blew out a long sigh. "I can barely believe Ben Rose was able to trace him here. Your father was so secretive that I doubt even a government agency could have found him." A faraway look came into the doctor's owlish brown eyes. "I'd like to think I would act differently now," he continued, "but at the time, your father was financially backing an institution I wanted to open..."

Alice's voice took on a faintly contemptuous edge. "So you owed him?"

Dr. Clark nodded. "The three of us who knew what happened all owed him, one way or another. And we were all sworn to secrecy." Staring at Dylan, the doctor shook his head. "What a pity. To think that all these years, you've gone without treatment, living cut off from the memory of what happened to you." He paused again, then continued, "Some psychiatrists would say not to tell you anything, they'd argue that you should undergo hypnosis, so your repressed memories could be slowly coaxed to the surface."

Alice said, "But not you?"

Dr. Clark shook his head adamantly. "No," he said. "Not under these circumstances, not when you're in danger." Before Dylan could respond, the doctor's gaze suddenly narrowed. "Wait a minute. If you have no memories of your brother, Mr. Devlyn, then how did you know you were twins?"

Dylan shrugged. "I didn't. Not until you said so." He guessed Santiago didn't know, either. Apparently, the detectives records weren't complete.

Dr. Clark's frown deepened. "But if you didn't know you and your brother were identical in appearance, or suspect that you were in danger, then what prompted you to undergo what must have been extreme plastic surgery?"

Dylan chewed his lower lip, considering. Without a doubt, his twin had somehow left this facility a year and a half ago and had attacked him the day of his wedding. No doubt, he'd left other times as well. After a long moment, Dylan finally said, "Uh, long story."

"Please, Dr. Clark," Alice chimed in. "Continue with what you were saying."

Dr. Clark shrugged. "From the psychiatric point of view, I always wore a coat of another color," he continued. "So I don't mind telling you what we know. And anyway, you are in danger. Extreme danger."

Alice's voice caught. "Extreme?"

Dr. Clark nodded. "Niles always showed aberrant tendencies. Stuart, you don't recall, but there were…incidents. Once, your father caught him suffocating you with a pillow in your room. Another time he cut you with a letter opener." Nodding toward Dylan's leg, the doctor said, "There's a scar on your calf, I believe."

There was. But all these years, Dylan thought he'd gotten it from a fall.

Registering Dylan's look of recognition, he went on, "Your brother's behavior was always marked by abusive acting out. Hitting. Using foul language he probably heard from your father's old rock-and-roll cronies, some of whom could be rough. At any rate, your father brought him to me early on, when he first started walking. Even then, he was exhibiting signs of aggression. And his eyes..." The doctor's voice trailed off.

Finally Alice said, "His eyes?"

The doctor shrugged. "Forgive me. I mean, this is certainly not a critical assessment. Nor is it something a trained professional should say. But his eyes..." Dr. Clark's shoulders lifted slightly, as if he was warding off a sudden chill. "They weren't...right. There was a gleam in them. Something malicious. Evil, even."

As abruptly as he'd risen, the doctor returned to the armchair and reseated himself. "When you were both five years old," he said, "he almost drowned you in the lake at the estate. Your father happened to look out the window of his study. Seeing what was happening, he ran out, but you were nearly dead. He pounded water from your lungs. Gave you mouth-to-mouth. But you were hard to resuscitate. Later, you were treated at Cedars Sinai Hospital, and it was clear you barely made it. Your heart had probably stopped, they said. You'd died and come back. Everybody thought it was an accident, of course."

Raising his gaze, the doctor smiled grimly. "Easy enough to explain, I suppose," he murmured. "You were a young child. You simply fell into the lake, not knowing how to swim. Besides, who in Hollywood would question Lang Devlyn?''

Alice sounded livid. "Not you."

He looked guilty as hell. "No, not me. God knows, better people than me are used to sliding things under the rugs for the rich and famous in Hollywood."

Somehow, it was hard for Dylan to find his voice. "And that's when my...my brother came here?"

The director nodded, then abruptly added, "While your mother was taking a trip abroad, Niles was brought to me. And later we told your mother Niles was dead."

Alice gasped. "Dead? My God, who would tell a mother that her son was dead?"

The director shrugged. "You don't understand. The child was thoroughly unrepentant. Niles only wanted another opportunity to kill his brother. He'd attempted it more than once. And it was intentional. Premeditated. He was five years old and yet he'd kill for something as simple as a toy. If Stuart was given gifts, or shown special attention, then the urge would come to..."

Kill.

There was a long silence.

Dr. Clark was staring beseechingly at Dylan. "Your father knew your mother would never agree to have him locked away. She couldn't accept the truth. And your father knew—" The director's gaze became more intense, his eyes piercing Dylan's. "That you'd eventually die." He sighed. "You can't blame her. What mother would believe such a thing about her boy? Even in the beginning, when Niles was brought to me, your mother refused to see his obvious problems. She kept saying his asocial behavior was something he'd outgrow.''

Dylan said, ''But she must have guessed something.''

''Lang Devlyn, your father, was a controlling and possessive man, especially when it came to your mother. But she was a bright woman. And she put two and two together. I don't think she ever really understood the truth, though I'd like to know if she did. At any rate, she sensed he was lying. Maybe she feared he'd done something to Niles, hurt him in some way. So, fearing for you, and unable to accept the truth about Niles, she fled.''

''Lang was trying to protect them,'' Alice said in a hushed voice.

Dr. Clark nodded. ''Right.''

''And Niles was brought here?'' Dylan clarified, trying to ignore the creepy feeling at the back of his neck. Somewhere on these premises was a man who possessed the face he used to have—the thick golden hair and cherubic round cheeks. A man who wanted him dead.

''No,'' Dr. Clark said. ''Actually, your brother was brought to another facility, the one I spoke of previously. He was transferred here, when I opened this place. Unfortunately I sometimes think the treatments have made him worse over the years. Not that there was an option for him other than institutional life.''

''He's worse?'' Dylan said.

''His hatred, like a cancer, has grown.'' Dr. Clark

sighed. "You see, that's the pathology. He's a real Jekyll and Hyde. Extremely dangerous and cunning. On the one hand, he's become increasingly obsessed with destroying you over the years. By accident or stealth, he's seen all his own records, of course. He blames your mother for abandoning him and your father for choosing you over him. Years ago, when Niles wasn't busy wanting you dead, he wanted to *be* you. And then..."

Alice gulped audibly. "Then?"

Dr. Clark's eyes were still on Dylan. "He became absolutely convinced he *is* you."

"*Is* me?" Dylan echoed.

"Yes. He's convinced. He goes into murderous rages when anything interferes with his fantasy. The jealousy he once felt has been internalized. And he's become the object he coveted most—you." Dr. Clark shook his head.

Dylan was still trying to process all this information. "He really thinks he's me?"

"More than thinks," Dr. Clark assured. "He believes it so deeply that sometimes he can't be swayed. Sometimes he believes it with every fiber of his being."

"Thank God he's locked up here," whispered Alice.

The director looked momentarily stunned. "I thought that was why you were here."

"What?" asked Dylan.

"Your brother escaped from here. Numerous times actually. Once about a year and a half ago. And then again about six months later. A few months ago..."

"He disappeared again?"

Dr. Clark nodded. "And now your father's been found murdered. We do our best here, and we have intense controls. Niles always comes back, but..."

"He gets out?" Alice said as if not really expecting a response.

Dr. Clark nodded. "I know he did it," he continued. "Niles felt such all-consuming blind rage for your father." Clasping his hands in his lap worriedly, Dr. Clark shrugged again. "I was out of town, and only heard the news of your father's death moments before you came in. I thought that's why you were here. Despite my promises to your father, I finally broke down and called the police. They have to know what's happening."

Alice and Dylan stared at each other.

Dr. Clark finally repeated, "I'm sure he killed your father."

There was another long pause. "You know," Dylan found himself saying, "there is something here that is even more disturbing."

"What could be more disturbing than this?" asked Dr. Clark.

Dylan could feel Alice's eyes riveted on his face. "If *Niles* Devlyn is absolutely convinced that he's *Stuart* Devlyn," Dylan began, "and if there's been some problem—don't ask me what—with the fingerprints we have—"

"Problem?" Alice interjected. "What kind of problem?"

"Well," Dylan said slowly. "We were twins,

babies, so who's to say that the right name is matched with the right print?''

Alice's gaze narrowed. ''What are you trying to say?''

''That if Niles is pathologically and completely convinced he's Stuart,'' Dylan repeated, ''and if I, too, believe myself to be Stuart, then maybe I'm really *Niles* Devlyn, and who knows what happened to Stuart.'' His eyes settled on Dr. Clark's. ''I could be Niles Devlyn,'' he repeated. ''Couldn't I?''

''If you had plastic surgery, yes.'' The man's eyes widened. ''Niles has been gone long enough to have had such a surgery…''

''Which means I could be Niles. And that I'm a killer.''

Chapter Twelve

"What do you mean? Go back to the hotel alone?" As Alice glanced through the thick-trunked, leafy trees toward the crowded parking lot, a sense of foreboding short-circuited her thoughts. She'd never seen anything like this place that was such a far cry from Wyoming. Here nature seemed too tightly controlled—bushes were trimmed to perfection, and flowers were surreally bright, as if everything had been filmed in Technicolor. All around her, countless sprinklers kept things unnaturally green in what rightfully should have been a desert.

She shuddered. The Highland Home, just like the rest of L.A., hid darker natures. It was beautiful—as long as one didn't look too closely. Alice scanned the trees again. She was wondering if a stranger was watching them, which might explain the creepy feeling, then she turned her attention to Dylan again. "You're not calling a cab, and I'm not going to the hotel alone. You're being totally ridiculous."

Shoving his hands into well-worn jeans that gently molded his thighs, Dylan surveyed her a long moment as if trying to discern the easiest method of getting his way. Not that he would. Her eyes lingered where his longish black hair brushed the collar of a pressed white shirt, and despite her determination to hold her ground, she had to fight not to touch the strands. Jerking his head in the direction of the stately white-columned building in the distance, he said, "C'mon, Alice. Weren't you listening in there? Didn't you hear what I said?"

"Of course I heard." She glanced away, putting a hand on her hip and shaking her head in anger. Her gaze returned to his. "But what you said was crazy. You are not Niles Devlyn."

His brown eyes looked darker than usual. Even in the bright sunlight, they seemed extraordinarily fixed and intent, as if he was ready to stare down cold hard reality, no matter how difficult or terrifying. "But I could be him. Dr. Clark said that's the pathology. Niles is totally convinced he's Stuart."

Her voice came out sounding more wounded than she intended. "Why are you doing this to me?"

He shot her an exasperated look. "Doing what?"

"You know what! You're pushing me away even if you don't know it."

"Of course I know it. It's intentional." He glared at her. "I'm trying to keep you alive."

"Maybe I don't want to be alive!"

Before the ridiculous, petulant words were out, he'd grabbed her, hauling her into his arms. Now his voice competed with hers for anger, though his was more controlled, holding an undercurrent of the emotion. "Don't ever say that, Alice."

She had no idea why she had, or what she'd really meant. But she couldn't live like this—not feeling consumed by lies and fear. And yet just feeling Dylan's arms so tightly around her made her chest feel too full. Tears pressured her eyes, and she damned herself for wanting to cry, then even more for wanting to melt against him. She did neither, but gazed into his eyes with furious impatience. No, she thought, she'd never forgive him for leaving her. If he loved her, he'd let her be involved in what was happening to him.

"Al," he sighed simply.

Her jaw set. "You're not Niles Devlyn, and you know it. I mean, I see your point, since he believes he's you. But—"

"But nothing. Don't you see what all this means?"

"All what?" Her voice caught, maybe from the argument, maybe from the embrace that made her remember the happier times when they'd been together. "We're getting so close to figuring all this out," she continued. "At the estate, you said your memory's coming back. And remember those calls you got in high school?"

Dylan nodded. "Yeah, I was thinking about them."

"Right. That could have been Niles. He could have called from here. Do you remember the voice? Was it distinctive, like yours?"

Dylan shrugged. "Darlin', that was years ago. And the voice was muffled. Like the guy was trying to disguise it."

"But was it like yours?" she repeated.

He considered, then shook his head. "As I said, I got those calls a long time ago."

"Maybe you did," she returned. "But I didn't. I got a call just minutes before you showed up in the driveway at the ranch. The man said he was you. He sounded like you." At the memory, terror tore at her heart, so much that she couldn't stop it from touching her voice. *Watch out, or you might cut yourself as you jump through the looking glass, Alice. And then you'll bleed.*

Dylan was studying her carefully, his eyes narrowing with concern. "You got a call? You didn't tell me?"

Maybe she should have. "He said he was you and that he wanted to kill me."

Dylan loosened his hands, sliding them slowly around her waist, as if checking to make sure she was okay. "What else? Tell me everything." After she did, he repeated, "Lord, why didn't you tell me?"

She fought against her returning temper, but knew he could read it in her eyes. "Tell you? When—night before last? You weren't exactly talking to me." Everything in his eyes said he wanted to remind her of why, so before he could, she added, "Because you'd so kindly taken it upon yourself to protect me, right?" Obviously, he didn't share the love she felt for him. Otherwise he'd realize how completely devastated she'd been...how sure he was dead.

Her voice trembled. "Yesterday I was thinking maybe Leland's jealousy of you drove him to..." Her voice trailed off. "But I guess not. I guess it's your brother's who's been..."

Stalking us.

Dylan's lips had slowly compressed into a tight line. After a moment they parted. "I can't believe you got a call."

"And the locket," she continued. "You were wearing that on our wedding day. You always wore it. Niles's escapes coincided with the wedding, and your time in Iowa."

"During the attack, the medallion was taken. Which means if he really attacked me, he took it."

"It all makes sense."

"Don't look so happy about it, Alice. I mean, if he's got the locket, then the blue bag is his. Since Clarisse identified me as carrying that bag, and since I no longer even look like my twin, then that means it was *me* who brought the bag to the motel. Maybe I've blocked it out. Maybe that's why I can't remember. Maybe I really did check in the Blue Sage—"

"Quit saying that!" Her eyes latched on to his. "Be honest. Do you remember checking into the motel with the bag?"

"No. I just said I didn't. That's the point. If I was Niles Devlyn I might not remember."

"You sound perfectly sane to me."

"So would Niles Devlyn."

Dawning apprehension filled her—and along with it, pure terror. "I don't believe you're Niles for an instant. But I do think he's been following you all along. I don't know how Clarisse mixed things up. Maybe Niles even paid her to lie. Whatever. The point is that Niles must have been steps behind you. He must be in Rock Canyon."

"Maybe."

Suddenly Alice felt sick. "He was at the wedding. Our wedding," she repeated. How horrible. During the happiest moment of their lives, while they'd been taking their vows, a killer had been watching and waiting...

"Alice?"

She realized her thoughts had trailed off. She'd been remembering that day—the sunshine and love, all the broken promises. Now Dylan was like a stranger to her. The old Dylan never would have pushed her away. He would have welcomed her help. Something had gone wrong with their love the moment he decided to leave the church without her. "He must have known about our wedding," she managed to continue, "and so he showed up to..."

"Hurt us?" Dylan said on another frustrated sigh. "Kill us? Separate us?" His eyes scanned her face, and sudden anger laced through his words. "God only knows what the psychotic bastard wants. Which is why I want to talk to the police, tell them everything. They'll put you under guard—"

"Your mother!" Alice said with a sudden gasp. "If he is in Rock Canyon, she needs to be guarded."

Dylan glanced away. "Or else I'm really Niles and I attacked her."

The words made her livid. *"Quit saying that!"* she repeated.

Brown eyes she'd once loved so much stared down into hers, breaking her heart. "When I was attacked..." He paused, glancing away as if searching for words. "I can't explain it," he said, his eyes returning to hers. "I had the strangest feeling. An odd sense of dislocation. Of dissociation. Like I was me, and yet, somehow not me. Like I was somebody else."

She stomped her foot. "You were being attacked, Dylan. I'm a nurse. And I can tell you right now that feeling could easily have been caused by rushes of noradrenaline."

"You mean adrenaline?"

"No. Noradrenaline. It numbs you. Helps you dissociate to minimize the trauma."

His eyes caught hers. "The same thing may have happened to me in the past." Slowly, he told her the little he recalled about the events at the lake.

Her heart welled with another kind of fear as he spoke. Dylan was so strong. His lean body snapped with whipcord strength—countless times she'd seen it strain while he roped cattle—and he was fearless when it came to confronting difficult issues. And yet he was more fragile than she'd ever imagined. More than life, she suddenly wanted to help him through this. She lifted a hand, but just before she could touch his cheek, he backed away.

"No, Alice," he said flatly, his eyes looking pained. "We can't be together. There's a chance that the lapses in my memory and my feelings of dislocation have occurred because I'm really Niles Devlyn. I'm going to the cops now, and they're going to protect you."

"From what?"

"From me."

"That's the most insane thing I've ever heard."

"Until this is solved, I can't risk hurting you. Or having you be hurt."

If nothing else, she guessed she had to admire his determination. "What are you going to tell the police?"

"Everything," he said. "Dr. Clark already called. Whoever he talked to probably took the information straight to Detective Santiago. So I'll go to him first. I'll tell him everything, including the fact that I'm really Dylan Nolan. Or that I think I am. I'll tell him I'm afraid I'm Niles, too. But that it seems as if I was attacked on our wedding day."

"It doesn't *seem*," Alice insisted. "It *is*."

"Maybe. But we can't risk it. Anyway, right now every piece of the puzzle has to be made available."

Realizing her heart had begun hammering too hard, she took a deep breath. "What if they lock you up? You know they're going to want to question you about Jan's murder."

"I'll tell them what I know."

"But you don't know anything. You didn't do it."

He sighed. "C'mon, Alice. You know going to the police is the right thing. And according to the news there was a child witness who said I killed Jan."

"But you didn't!" Risking Dylan's being locked up hardly seemed right to Alice. "Please," she pressed. "Do you really think you're Niles Devlyn, and that you might have killed your father? Or Jan?"

"I don't know."

A male voice came from the trees. "I do."

It was Santiago. Both Alice and Dylan turned toward him, just as two more uniformed officers appeared.

"Detective Santiago," Dylan said simply.

The detective nodded. "We headed over as soon as Dr. Clark called. We've also recovered tapes from some more hidden surveillance cameras on the grounds of the estate. Dr. Clark just confirmed that you've had surgery and no longer look like yourself, though fingerprints identify you as Stuart Devlyn." The detective heaved a world-weary sigh. "I don't know what to make of all this, but I do know one thing."

Alice didn't much like his tone. "Which is?"

"That whoever he is—" Santiago nodded at Dylan. "He's under arrest. The surveillance cameras show him on the estate grounds on the day of Lang Devlyn's murder."

Dylan's voice remained exceedingly calm. "I have no recollection of ever going there before today, when Alice and I spoke to Ben Rose."

Santiago nodded thoughtfully. "Well, you don't seem to recall a lot of things, now, do you, Mr. Devlyn? And that might add credence to your own theory, most of which I just overheard, that you're really Niles, not Stuart, Devlyn."

"That's *crazy!*" Alice emphasized adamantly.

Santiago shrugged. "I always let the D.A. ponder questions of sanity. He loves mind games. Me, I just lock up bad guys. Right now I've got proof on video that you—" he nodded toward Dylan again "—were on the grounds of the estate."

Something in Alice gave. Without even thinking,

she edged back a step. Suddenly, she heard with real clarity what the detective was saying. Despite his verbal claims to the contrary, Dylan *had* been at the estate on the day of his father's murder. Clarisse *had* seen him check into the motel, carrying the blue nylon bag which contained Alice's picture. The ring bearer had said he killed Jan, though he would have looked different then. Suddenly she wasn't so sure she knew the truth. She stared at him. It was hard to believe— no, impossible to believe—that this man was Niles Devlyn. He was so like Dylan...

But he would be. They're twins, Alice.

Moments ago, she'd been so sure this couldn't be true. But now her stomach churned and bile rose in her throat. *What do they always say?* she thought in panic. *The body doesn't lie. But what if it had? What if she was wrong last night? Dear God, what if he really is Niles Devlyn...what if I made love to a murderer?*

"Really?" he was saying to Santiago. "Are you sure my picture was on the video cameras? I was really there the day my father was murdered?"

"The tapes show the whole thing," returned Santiago.

He said, "Whole thing?"

"Yes," affirmed Santiago. "The murder. From start to finish. How you stabbed your father thirty-two times." Santiago turned away in disgust as the two uniformed officers came closer. "'See him bleed,'" Santiago muttered. "That's what you kept saying on the tape while you killed him. 'See the poor bastard bleed.'"

SHE'S MINE, all mine now. Oh, my sweet little wife. Very soon, we'll get to see you bleed.

He watched Alice from a car in the parking lot. She was as pretty as ever, as pretty as a picture, with the light California breeze making the hem of her sunflower sundress sway. No one could have looked more sweet and innocent.

Or so...confused. She turned this way, then that. Just staring around, clutching the shoulder strap of her handbag. The keys to the rental car were now dangling from her hand—she'd just taken them from her bag. But she couldn't get inside her car, not yet. Instead, her eyes were still riveted on the police officers leading Niles Devlyn away.

Inside the car, he sighed with relief. "Niles Devlyn," he muttered, shaking his head. "My brother definitely ought to be locked up." Oh, yes. Shame on him. He was a murderer, after all. A cold-blooded killer who took such pride in his work. And now the cops had finally figured it out.

Which was good, since now Alice would be all his.

Hunkered down in the seat of the stolen car, he peered through the windshield, then reached up and adjusted the rearview mirror. No cops behind him. Good. He wouldn't want them accidentally noticing him now. That might raise a few eyebrows.

He raised his own in the rearview mirror, and then he felt suddenly odd. As if he were seeing everything from a vantage point that was underwater. As if nothing was quite real.

Stuart Devlyn stared back from the mirror.

Or Dylan Nolan.

Or whatever you wanted to call him. Scum of the earth. Bastard. Scourge.

He continued staring at himself. Gone were the cherubic cheeks, the thick wavy golden sun-kissed locks of hair. Tilting his head, he listened for a long moment, hearing an undercurrent of something dark sliding through his blood. He could almost hear the words that dark voice wanted to speak…

Words that were wicked.

And evil.

Because suddenly, he wasn't Stuart Devlyn at all. Why in the world had he been thinking he was Stuart? No, he was Niles Devlyn, wasn't he?

"Yes," he murmured. "I think I am."

A breathy insane chuckle escaped his lips. Oh, yes…he could remember now. Shutting his eyes, he saw red. The red of the sun as it bled into the sky on hot summer nights. The red of apples. Cherries.

And blood.

That was the best red of all.

Definitely, he was Niles Devlyn. And now he could remember things—attacking his brother in the church on his wedding day, making calls to him, years ago, from an office phone at the Highland Home. Wrecking their mother's credit from the office computer.

Not to mention beating her…hurting her. And killing Jan Sawyer.

Giggling, he simply couldn't believe it. *He* was in this car. And *Stuart* was going to jail!

What a coup. But following Stuart to Iowa had been the best idea. There'd been no greater pleasure than leaving the Highland Home again. Ha! The place had the most lax security money could buy. Finding the plastic surgeon had been easy. So had getting him to duplicate the same surgery he'd given Stuart, and then killing the doctor.

It had been a thrill to see the bandages come off. Oh...the pain of those few days when Niles and his twin looked so different. When Niles still possessed cherubic round cheeks and golden hair. And Stuart or Dylan had those enviable dark good looks. Niles Devlyn glanced into the rearview mirror again, at his long dark hair, full lips and brown eyes.

Their father's eyes.

Yes, Lang Devlyn had possessed the same liquid, dreamy eyes. At least until he'd died. In death, they'd become something so much more interesting. Darker, wider and terror-filled. As he'd died, Dad had looked so...*alive.*

Loosing a soft, satisfied moan of pure pleasure that warmed him to his bones, Niles imagined his father's wounds.

See him bleed.

Niles had watched, gleefully following as his father dragged himself over the marble floors, holding the wounds while the blood ran through his fingers. How ridiculously futile that gesture had been. Niles sighed again. People could be so crazy....

His eyes shifted to the windshield, settling on Alice again. The plainclothes detective had already gotten into the unmarked car, and the two uniformed cops had already seated Stuart into the caged back seat of the marked vehicle. A siren swooped once.

Looking vaguely uncertain, Alice now opened the

door of the rental car. A moment later, Niles turned the key in the ignition of his ride. Not that he needed to follow her.

He already knew she was staying at a high-rise hotel called the Sunset Arms in Beverly Hills. The police would probably be posted outside her room, too. But that didn't really bother Niles. *People* never really bothered Niles Devlyn.

And if they bothered him too much, he simply killed them.

He didn't care if they were cops, either. Hatred surged within him. He didn't pause to question what it meant or where it came from. Probably it had begun deep in the womb, when it was determined that he would be born without his own face.

A twin.

A replica. A duplicate. The son who came into being second—on the heels of a brother. The son who, consequently, had nothing. Not the mother. Not the wife. Not the job on the fancy ranch.

But all that was about to change.

Because he was about to have Alice.

His eyes were still glued to her. Now he could see the back of her blond head peeking above the headrest. As she pulled out, he followed, imagining how lovely her pale skin was going to look, covered with so many bright red beautiful slashes.

Chapter Thirteen

"Stop the car." Tearing his gaze from the wire screen between the front and back seats, Dylan wrenched around, his heart racing, his eyes riveted on Alice. Why hadn't he listened to his gut? Given what Dr. Clark said, it made sense that Dylan might be Niles—it had to be considered—but Dylan hadn't really believed he was someone other than himself, not deep down.

Especially not when he'd *seen* Niles.

"C'mon," Dylan growled. "You've got to stop."

This time the young dark-haired rookie on the passenger side turned and said, "No can do."

"Damn," Dylan muttered. Santiago had just pulled out of the parking lot when Dylan turned to look at Alice—and found himself staring right at his twin brother. A straight, unbroken line could have been drawn between them, and the sudden connection was terrifying. In a heartbeat, Dylan understood: Niles was still his look-alike. He'd followed Dylan, duplicated the plastic surgery, then killed the surgeon.

Because he's insane.

Not that Dylan could see the maniacal glimmer in Niles's eyes—he was too far away—but Dylan could swear he felt it. The man had killed repeatedly in cold blood: Jan Sawyer, the surgeon, and Lang Devlyn. He'd attacked their mother and fantasized about murdering Alice, judging from the phone calls and what he'd done to her picture.

In the heartbeat when their eyes connected, memories flooded Dylan. He was swinging, staring down, flying toward the ground, the dew-wet, fresh-cut grass rushing up. His daddy was inside the house. And he loved his daddy, who played guitar and piano, and who sang him songs at night as he and his brother went to sleep. But he could never understand why his brother was so jealous.

"You get everything," Niles said while they were swinging.

"Do not."

"Do, too."

"Do not." Why couldn't his brother just act normal? "Wanna race me to the house?"

"Sure."

The two golden-haired boys jumped from the swings and ran for the house, but they never made it. On the way, Niles grabbed him and pushed him into the lake, under the water. Now he relived every terrifying moment—plunging into the icy water, losing consciousness. Right before he went under, he smelled that cloying scent: the mixture of oleander and wet leaves. He could smell cinders, too, from summer brushfires down in the canyons. He'd remembered that smell during the attack at the wedding, and he'd remembered the feel of a hand wrapping around his throat. Now he knew it was Niles's hand. And when he'd look up, toward the lake's surface, it had been Niles's face staring down at him, not his own.

He punched the back of the seat. "Pull over!"

Behind them, Alice's rental car dropped back a block, and now Niles Devlyn's blue car turned a corner, following. Quickly, Dylan scanned the back seat. There were no door handles, no objects he could use to knock out a window or windshield. The windows were rolled up. How could he get out of here, run back and warn Alice? "You've got to stop. He's a killer."

"He who?" said the driver. He was old—bald with gray whiskers and a paunch. He looked as if he were hours from retirement, and hardly about to put himself in the line of fire.

"Niles Devlyn," Dylan snarled, his heart skipping a beat as the cops turned a corner, making them lose sight of the other two cars. "My...brother."

Brother. It sickened him to use that word.

The cop in the passenger seat stared through the wire-mesh screen and the back windshield. "Huh?" he said. "I don't see anybody."

"He was behind us. He looks like me." Dylan glanced back, his eyes scanning the street. Had Niles caught up to Alice? Rammed her car from the back, maybe? Gotten out and—

Relief flooded him when he saw Alice's car turn the corner. Thank God she was still okay. "There. Back behind Alice. He's in the blue car."

"Look," the driver muttered. "I don't know anything about this case. We're just 'sposed to take you in for questioning. If there's really somebody—''

"Stop the car!"

"Mister, we—"

"She's in *danger*."

"She who?"

Letting his anger show would make the cops less likely to listen, so Dylan kept his voice tightly controlled. "Alice. She's—"

"Take it up with Santiago down at the station," the rookie in the passenger seat said.

Dylan wanted to scream, but he settled for speaking through clenched teeth. "The man's a murderer. The man's—"

"Like I said, when we get to the sta—"

"Use your radio, dammit," Dylan choked out urgently. "Make someone intercept her car. It's that tan Buick. It's a rental."

Nobody reached for the radio.

"You're endangering a woman's life!" Dylan's eyes kept scanning the back seat; surely there was something here with which he could knock out a window. "He's a murderer. Don't you see? He looks like me now. That's why I'm on the video cameras at the estate. He killed our father—"

"Your father?"

"Don't you know anything about this case?"

The driver shook his head.

The rookie turned and shot Dylan a peeved glance. "No offense, but we get this kind of thing—"

"Thing?"

"Yeah, thing. You know, one guy saying the other

guy did it. Or claiming the real perp's in a vehicle behind us."

"He *is* behind us."

The driver said, "It'll be better all 'round if you just sit back and enjoy the ride."

"Enjoy the ride!" Dylan snapped, his neck craning. Alice had dropped back yet another block. She was usually a slow, cautious driver, and right now she was no doubt battling her own confusion and concern. He could barely stand to remember the dawning look on her face as Santiago talked.

She really thinks I'm a murderer now. That alone made fury boil inside him. So did the thwarted need to protect her. What if she wound up going back to the hotel instead of following them to the police station? What if Niles tailed her to the room and—

Dylan couldn't stand to imagine Alice's pale skin red with slashes, her lovely green eyes slits of terror. Lord, Niles had stabbed their father thirty-two times. He'd murdered Jan! Feeling as if he was losing his mind, Dylan succinctly said, "For God's sake, you two, I am not making this up." Some blocks back, Alice was turning a corner. Both she and Niles were following the cop car onto a two-lane road now, headed for the freeway.

There was no hope if Dylan didn't do something. He had to escape. Somehow, he had to get out of the car, away from these two cops.

But Alice was so impossibly far away now. Sunlight glinted off the tan car's windshield, silhouetting her inside the front seat. She was sitting ramrod straight; he imagined her hands were frozen and gripping the steering wheel. He couldn't begin to imagine what was going through her mind. Even though she couldn't see his face from here, or read his expression, Dylan tried waving his arms, hoping to get her attention. At least they hadn't handcuffed him. Yet.

Not that she noticed him waving. Maybe she didn't want to notice.

She really does think I'm a cold-blooded killer. The thought made Dylan queasy. The driver put on a turn signal, and as he swerved onto the freeway, everything seemed to be happening in slow motion. Dylan's heart hammered. There were six lanes of traffic now. They were going to lose Alice! Dylan's eyes darted frantically across the miles of concrete. Tan cars were everywhere. Blue ones, too.

Where's Alice? For a second, everything felt offkilter; Dylan was a child again, listening to his mother read *Curious George.* Over and over, she'd point at the pictures, saying, "Where's George?"

What a helluva thing to remember now. Dylan stared at the bumper-to-bumper traffic, his chest squeezing tighter and tighter. He'd lost Alice, but Niles Devlyn hadn't. No doubt, the killer was right behind her.

Dylan's eyes fell to his steel-toed boots. Maybe… Using the toe of one boot against the heel of the other, he slipped his foot out. If he was fast, maybe he could use the steel toe to knock out a window, then grab the exterior door handle and open the door.

The invisible bands around his chest suddenly tightened, making him feel breathless, as if he was suffocating. Drowning. Memories of the cold dark water threatened to engulf him again. *You have to fight.*

This time, his twin wouldn't win.

He watched the traffic. If they slowed down, he'd be ready. He might only get one chance. The two cops in the front seat were carrying guns, and he sized the men up, wondering if he could wrestle a gun away from one of them, so he'd have protection when he confronted Niles.

If he confronted Niles.

He still couldn't see either car. But the hotel was close to the police station. Even if Alice went to the hotel, maybe Dylan could get there before Niles. If only he could escape. He stared at the traffic again.

There! When he saw Alice, relief flooded him.

But only for a second. Because his twin brother was right behind her.

SHE'D COME STRAIGHT to the hotel.

Maybe she shouldn't have, maybe she should have gone to the police station, but she had to be alone. To think. And anyway, a policeman had met her here, and now for some hours, he'd been posted outside the door.

They wouldn't say why.

It didn't make sense, since Dylan was under lock and key. But he'd tried to escape. Detective Santiago had called. He'd said that, on the freeway, Dylan had attempted to break the window in the back seat of the cop car, not realizing the glass was shatter-proof.

As if Alice cared to hear details. She'd had to confront the fact that she'd made love to a killer. Wasn't that vile enough for one day? Bile rose in her throat. She choked it down. With everything in her power, she tried not to think back, or remember how she'd felt when she'd first seen Dylan, injured in the ranch's driveway.

Had that only been two days ago?

It seemed like another lifetime. "I wish it was somebody else's lifetime," she whispered. And yet she could still remember how, when she'd first gazed into Dylan's eyes, her heart had stopped—and then flooded with joy. *Dylan!* she'd thought. It was a miracle! He'd come back into her life. He was disguised, but he wasn't dead as she'd imagined. He was safe. She'd been so sure there was a reasonable explanation for where he'd been, and why he'd returned.

Now she shuddered. The explanation was that Dylan was also a man named Stuart or Niles Devlyn. Who knew—or cared—which twin he really was? Certainly not Alice. She'd quit trying to understand this puzzle. She was too scared and her heart was too broken. Maybe the twins' fingerprints had gotten mixed up.

Either way, it was Dylan who'd had plastic surgery, and who'd been identified as Lang Devlyn's killer. Clarisse had also seen him at the Blue Sage Motel, carrying the bag that contained the locket. Thinking of the locket and phone calls, Alice shuddered. *Why didn't he just kill me?*

"C'mon," she whispered shakily. "Ten deep breaths." She managed to get hold of herself long enough to take two. Somehow, she'd get through this.

At least that's what she'd told herself for the last hour, during her bath.

Now, from where she stood in the hotel bedroom, she stared at her reflection in the full-length mirror of the open bathroom door. Right now, she couldn't even stand to look at herself. *I slept with a killer. I felt his hands on me. I let him—*

No longer able to bear the thoughts, Alice cut them off. Turning, she pulled a bathrobe from her carry-on, then tugged it over the silk gown she was already wearing.

"How am I going to sleep tonight?" she said, her voice still shaking. Her hands were shaking, too, she noticed. She stared down at them; her long pale fingers suddenly looked so weak. Finding a hairbrush, she lifted it, then began pulling it through her wet, tangled hair.

At least the room was nice. Spacious and calming in its unobtrusiveness. Two queen-size beds were side by side. Exactly alike—like twins—they were neatly covered with matching peach spreads. Elsewhere things were beige—the thick carpeting, the light paint on the walls, the plush bathroom towels.

Alice glanced nervously toward the door.

She didn't know why she bothered to look. Of course the chain lock was still on. She'd already checked at least five times.

But it didn't matter.

It would never matter.

She couldn't imagine anything making her feel safe again. She'd made love to a killer. Invited him into her home. Wanted him to kiss her...touch her. Oh

God! It was so sick. Why hadn't she known? Why hadn't she asked more questions? Why hadn't she sensed the truth? Why had she so easily become his victim?

No, she could never feel safe again, not when her own body and thoughts had betrayed her. Not when she'd been so sure she'd found Dylan again, and that Dylan could never kill.

But he had.

And it *was* him, that much she knew. He'd known things only Dylan could—such as their special spot at Cat's Canyon. Which meant he'd changed his face, just as he'd claimed. In turn, that meant it was his face—not his brother's—that Santiago saw on the tapes from the estate.

She still couldn't believe it.

"Santiago saw him kill Lang Devlyn," she whispered. *In cold blood.* She shivered again, and a creepy prickly feeling crawled down her spine like something vile. Like spiders.

Wherever he was, Niles Devlyn would still look like the old Dylan, with rounder cheeks and straight, fine golden hair. No doubt he was criminally insane, just as Dr. Clark claimed. He'd been locked up for years. But now it was clear that murderous impulses ran in the Devlyn genes. Because Niles's brother Stuart—or rather Dylan—was definitely a killer, too.

Twins.

Two insane killers.

Poor Nancy Nolan. If she fully recovered from her coma, how would Nancy live with this? Realizing she'd paused in midstroke, and that her fingers had wrapped icily around the hairbrush, Alice clenched her teeth as if they were about to chatter. Somehow, she forced the brush through her hair again. If she could just keep moving, maybe things would be fine.

But she knew that was a lie.

She'd taken a hot bath anyway, knowing that a thousand baths couldn't make her feel clean. No, she felt dirty. Filthy, she amended. How could she have let such a sick creature touch her? How could she have let him—

She loosed a sudden sob. The second it came from her throat, she clamped her lips shut. For a second, the walls she'd thrown up around her heart threatened to come down. Not that she'd let them. She felt too betrayed. Too confused.

Too damn scared.

And somehow she was sure she'd never feel—really feel—again. She felt too numb inside. Certainly she'd never trust herself to love again. Not after realizing she'd loved a murderer.

And she had loved him!

She'd been mad because he'd left her. But she'd started to feel so ready to forgive him. She'd started to fantasize that she and Dylan could start anew.

She slipped the hairbrush into the pocket of her bathrobe, then continued staring at herself in the mirror. Who was this woman who was so easily fooled? It was as if she'd never even seen herself before. Her eyes drifted down the robe and gown set to her pale knees and calves. How could she have let a killer touch her? Let him kiss her mouth? Enjoyed the feel of his breath on her cheeks? Feeling bile rise in her throat again, she tensed.

Just as she was about to run for the toilet, the phone rang.

She jumped, feeling startled, the shrill double ring going right into her blood. Turning numbly from her reflection, she stared at the phone. It rang again. Only then did she walk toward the bedside table between the beds to pick it up.

"Hello?"

"Can you...hear me...Ms. Eastman?"

Barely. The line was breaking up. A high-pitched tone cut through static. "Who is this?"

"Detective..."

She thought he said Santiago. "What?" She raised her voice. "Who is this? Is this Detective Santiago? Are you there?"

"Sorry, it's a cell phone. I'm in the car."

Flinty anger coursed through her. Whatever he was going to say, she didn't want to hear it. She just wanted to get away from here. To get on the very next plane out of Los Angeles and home to the ranch.

Couldn't the detective understand? She'd been tricked into loving a killer! Somehow she had to get help and heal herself. She needed time and space. Nature. Long walks in the woods. Maybe a good shrink. And then maybe—God knew how—she might be able to move on with her life. Santiago was saying something she couldn't understand. "What?" Alice said into the mouthpiece.

"I said..."

"What?" she said again.

"He escaped."

A free hand rose to her gown, covering the spot over her heart. Weakening, her knees buckled, and she sat on the edge of one of the beds. "From jail?" she managed to say.

"Yes, he…"

The rest was lost to static. "It's supposed to be secured in there," she gasped in a strangled voice. "They're locked up. Those guys are in *cells*. You do put them in cells, don't you? How could—"

"He got loose on the way to the dining hall." Santiago's voice suddenly came clear. "Sit tight," he continued. "We're on our way. We'll be right there."

We'll be right there.

Her heart pounded. Dear Lord, they were on their way to help her! That could mean only one thing— they thought Dylan was coming here. She froze. Her fingers, already icy, were curled tightly around the receiver. She concentrated on trying to let go, but she couldn't. The phone stayed frozen to her hand because she was so scared.

He killed Lang Devlyn, she thought. He killed the plastic surgeon who operated on his face. He almost killed his mother. He killed Jan.

And now he's coming to kill me.

Someone pounded on the door.

Her eyes shot to it. Santiago? she wondered. Could he have made it here so soon? It didn't seem likely. But she was in a state of panic. Her body and mind were numb from denial and fear. Maybe more time had passed than she thought.

The pounding sounded again.

A cop. Relief flooded her. Surely it was the cop outside the door. Of course it was. Detective Santiago had probably contacted him on his radio, and the police officer wanted to talk to her, to assure her. Turning, she didn't even bother to hang up the phone. When her fingers unclenched, she let the receiver slide down to the mattress, then she bolted for the door.

She looked through the peephole.

She couldn't see his face—his chin was tilted down—but she could clearly see the bill of his uniform cap, the blue of his suit and the badge pinned to his shirt pocket. Another wave of relief rushed through her. "Yes?"

He knocked again. She guessed he figured she couldn't hear him through the door. She quickly unhooked the chain latch and pulled the knob.

She gasped as the door swung open.

Dylan stared back, smiling.

He was dressed in the police officer's uniform. Her eyes flitted toward the fire door at the end of the hallway, and she was sure Dylan had killed the officer and dragged him to the stairwell. How else could Dylan have gotten his clothes?

And then she realized she couldn't move.

She was frozen.

Not even her fingers would move. They were splayed at her sides, and there was nothing she could do.

I have to move or I'm going to die.

Dylan tilted his head. His smile broadened. And

then, with sudden terrifying precision, his hand thrust out, backhanding her. The blow lifted her off her feet.

She staggered back like a drunk as he entered the room. The door slammed shut, and a knife came from nowhere. It appeared in a black-gloved hand, flashing a terrifying silver.

He grinned. "I can't wait to cut you up."

Dear God, move, Alice!

As he stepped closer, something inside her rolled over. She felt a strange sense of doubt she was powerless to deny. Even now, she couldn't quite believe what she'd been trying to convince herself of for hours. Even now, when she saw the knife in his hand, she couldn't really believe Dylan was a killer.

He'd never hurt me!

Memories pushed at her frozen consciousness. How they'd met outside the general store. How he'd made love to her that first time in the grass in Cat's Canyon. Surely this couldn't be the same man…

"Ready to go through the looking glass, Alice?" He loosed a high-pitched hysterical-sounding giggle that chilled her already icy blood. "When you go through the looking glass, look out, 'cause I think you're gonna get cut." He took another step, and she somehow she managed to stagger back between the beds and toward the phone. The dial tone changed to a sound indicating it was off the hook.

"I'm going to watch you bleed." He raised his voice. "You like to bleed, don't you, Alice?" Taking another slow step, he tilted his head and studied her, deciding where to make the first cut.

Why won't my body come unstuck?

She was half crouched in the two-foot space between the beds now, poised between fight and flight, with him still approaching. There were weapons: a heavy lamp behind her. The phone receiver. The hairbrush in her pocket. If she could only move.

"You wore a white gown for me. Is that a wedding dress, little wife? Or a nightie? Maybe you want a little something else before I kill you. Some hanky-panky, Alice?"

Lord, she had to move!

He swung the knife right in front of her face. Quickly, its silver flash arched past the front of her gown, then slashed across her forearm.

She could only stare down at the gaping hole in the sleeve of her robe, at the thin red line of blood rising on the fabric.

"That's right, little wife. Time to make your white dress bloody."

Bloody.

The word reverberated. She watched helplessly as his hand came up—poised and high, the already bloody tip of the knife aimed right at her face. *Bastard!* Had he said these vile words to Jan? To Lang Devlyn? To the poor surgeon he'd killed?

Alice moved before she even felt the supercharge that surged through her like liquid lightning. Her eyes widened. Oxygen rushed her. Her mind snapped into hyper-alertness. Heightened senses picked up scents: his citrus aftershave, tobacco clinging to the uniform.

Her hand shot up. Her fingers squeezed around his wrist with such superhuman strength that he cried out. He tried to wrench away, but he couldn't move.

He offered a wicked laugh. "Oh, wife of mine," he said, "I like this. I like it when you fight dirty."

"Good," she snapped. "Dylan, you deserve everything you get."

"Dylan?" he said.

She barely registered the word as she grabbed the knife. Maybe she'd been fool enough to love him. But she'd kill him now if she had to. Looking stunned, he swiped at the knife. Catching it for an instant, he nearly plunged it into her chest. But she turned it around, and before he could react drove it into his belly. Horrified, she gasped and let go as blood spurted onto her gown.

"Alice?" he said.

She could barely believe what she'd done. Had she really stabbed Dylan? One look, and she knew the wound would be fatal. She watched as he backed away, talking as he stepped between the beds, looking strangely confused.

"Alice?" he said again.

Something in her gave. She took a step toward him. But then remembered: this wasn't Dylan. Not really. It simply couldn't be the man she'd loved. From now on, she'd pretend he'd been somebody else.

She watched as his hand closed over the handle of the knife that was stuck in his belly. "From now on," she found herself saying aloud, forcing herself to look into those insane eyes, "I'll think of you as two different men. The man I loved." She stared at him, still unable to believe she'd ever loved this man. "And the monster I just killed."

The insane eyes looked glazed now. A bubble of

blood appeared on his lips. But his head snapped up, as if he'd heard someone coming. He screamed—a loud blood-curdling cry—and then wrenched the knife from deep in his belly. With the knife dripping blood, he rushed toward Alice.

Instinctively, she lifted her hands to shield her face just as the door opened. She barely heard. Suddenly everything seemed to move in slow motion. The knife came an inch closer to her face, then another inch, aimed right at her eyes.

And then it stopped.

She realized someone grabbed Dylan from behind. Glancing past him, she expected to see Santiago. And she did, though he was at the doorway, along with the cop who'd previously been posted outside. Closer, the man who'd grabbed her attacker was...

"Dylan?" she gasped.

He glanced from his brother to her. "It's me, Alice."

She stared. Her mind simply couldn't catch up. Somehow Niles Devlyn had duplicated the surgery Dylan had! Her heart flooded with emotion. How could she not have trusted him? Would he ever forgive her? She understood now the extreme danger he'd been trying to protect her from. Her voice was a mere croak. "Dylan?" she said again.

Dylan didn't respond, only said, "He's almost gone."

IT WAS STRANGE to hold him. The body was so exactly like his own in size, strength and shape. Dylan backed away, slowly bringing his brother to the floor. He hated him. And yet he didn't...couldn't.

He'd feel differently if things had turned out some other way. But Alice was alive. And this man was criminally insane. He was all there was left of a family—a father and a brother—that Dylan had never known. Gently, he finished laying his dying brother on the floor. Lowering himself, Dylan moved Niles's head and rested it on his thigh, then Dylan stared down...

Into what looked like his own face.

Strange, he thought. It was as if he were watching himself die. Niles stared up, his filmy eyes barely focused. He was trying to say something.

Dylan leaned closer. "What?"

"You had everything," Niles whispered with effort.

Dylan thought of them, as boys, swinging by the lake. *Do not,* he'd said.

Do, too.

Dylan watched as his brother's eyes shut, then opened again. "You...you..."

When his brother could say nothing more, Dylan forced himself to finish, "I have everything?"

"Yes..." Clearly, it had become too difficult to speak. No lights had lived in Niles Devlyn's eyes for years. But whatever life had been there was finally burning out. His sudden, soft gasp sounded like a last breath. And then, the second before he died, Niles Devlyn whispered, "You have Alice."

Lifting a hand, Dylan closed his brother's eyes. Then he raised his gaze to Alice's. Tear-filled eyes latched on to his, and he could see the love in them, the knowledge and forgiveness. She understood the danger now. She'd faced it down herself, plunging in the knife that had killed Niles. She understood that Dylan would go to any lengths to protect her—now and forever.

You have Alice.

Dylan could still hear the words. And the first peace he'd felt in a long time descended on him. "I do," he said simply, looking into her eyes.

"Yes," she returned softly. "You do."

When he glanced away—just as Santiago and his men came closer—Dylan caught a glimpse of himself and his brother in the mirror on the open bathroom door. Somehow, seeing himself and his brother reflected together, told him it was really over. He and his brother really were two different people. The nightmares had ended. His childhood memories were restored.

And yes, he thought, his eyes lifting to Alice's, which were so alive and green, like grass in summer. He had Alice. And she would always be his.

Epilogue

"We should head back to the ranch," Alice said as her eyes scanned their special spot in Cat's Canyon.

"Hmm." Standing with his arm around her thickening waist, Dylan took in the rolling meadow, then looked into Alice's eyes again. They were so lovely, the exact color of the grass, and her pale skin was tinged a faint pink from the summer sun. She was pregnant, too. A blue silk maternity dress fluttered around her knees in the wind. He smiled. "You don't really want to go home, do you?" he asked, his eyes straying suggestively to a nearby tree. "I mean, it's so secluded and quiet here that we could..."

"Dylan." There was mock censure in her eyes. "We've got to go home."

"Tired of my company?"

Alice feigned a yawn. "You always put me to sleep."

He grinned. "I have my ways."

She laughed. "You sure do."

Leaning, she ran a playful hand through his hair. Some days he wondered if he'd ever get used to his new face, but it was definitely nice to have his hair growing back. Without the dye and perm, it was coming in straight and golden-blond again.

It was one of many things that seemed to have gotten back to normal. His mother's health was fine. She'd been out of the hospital for months, and had coped with surprising fortitude. For years, she'd doubted her decision to flee from Lang Devlyn and she'd felt guilty about not telling Dylan the truth. But now she was sure she'd done the most protective thing a mother could, though she wished she'd known her other son had been alive. When Niles broke into her home and attacked her, he'd told her where he'd been over the years. Contrary to what Dr. Clark claimed, Nancy felt she could have accepted the truth in the past, but that her possessive husband had made it virtually impossible for her to do so.

In Los Angeles, the Devlyn case had been tied up within hours. Sheriff Sawyer had found his old files and Dylan's fingerprints, and he'd called Detective Santiago just as Dylan escaped, to say Dylan Nolan and Stuart Devlyn were the same man. At the time, the detective had located the trucker with whom Dylan had hitched a ride into Rock Canyon, and who verified Dylan's story. The officer who'd been posted outside Alice's hotel room had recovered easily from wounds that had been superficial, too. No one knew why Niles hadn't killed the man. After all, he had killed so many.

Dylan had shipped his twin's body to Rock Canyon. And now Niles Devlyn was buried in the local cemetery. It was something Dylan felt he had to do. Because he'd been haunted by elusive memories for so many years, Dylan had no intention of forgetting anything these days—good or bad. Having his brother buried here was a gentle reminder of their personal history. And when he passed the cemetery, he often felt a rush of gratitude: for his mother's health. For Alice and the coming baby.

Months ago he and Alice had remarried, and their first child was well on the way. Which meant Dylan didn't dwell much on the millions he'd inherited from his father's estate. In fact, it hadn't changed their lives one bit. He had all the riches he'd ever need right here in Rock Canyon.

Still gazing at Alice, Dylan suddenly smiled. Another strange turn was that the case brought Leland into contact with Clarisse at the Blue Sage Motel. The two were Rock Canyon's latest hot item now, and Dylan and Alice were pretty sure it would turn out to be more.

Dylan guessed he could hardly blame Leland for his possessiveness when it came to Alice. Damn if Dylan didn't feel twinges of the emotion himself. And after talking things out, he and Leland had started seeing eye-to-eye. Enough so that they were jointly running the Eastman ranch. It was even easier, since Leland and Alice had patched things up—as friends, and Leland had even sought some help in dealing with his anger. Besides which, once Alice was out of danger, Leland's temper had calmed.

"I'm not kidding," Alice said now. "Our mothers are expecting us for dinner, you know."

Dylan rolled his eyes playfully and tugged Alice

down into the grass. "And us," he teased. "We're simply expecting."

Looping her arms around his neck, she rolled so that she lay on top of him, her full belly pressuring his. "We are."

His smiled broadened. "Hmm. What are you expecting?"

"To spend the rest of my life with you."

Dylan laughed softly. As his mouth sought hers, he whispered, "That's what I like about the greatest expectations, Alice."

"What's that?" she murmured against his lips.

He sighed before delivering a gentle, loving kiss. "That when I'm with you, they always come true."

Amnesia...
an unknown danger...
a burning desire.

With

HARLEQUIN®

I N T R I G U E®

you're just

A MEMORY AWAY

from passion, danger...and love!

**Look for all the books in this
exciting miniseries:**

#527 ONE TEXAS NIGHT
by Sylvie Kurtz
August 1999

#531 TO SAVE HIS BABY
by Judi Lind
September 1999

#536 UNDERCOVER DAD
by Charlotte Douglas
October 1999

A MEMORY AWAY—where remembering
the truth becomes a matter of life,
death...and love!

Available wherever Harlequin books are sold.

HARLEQUIN®
Makes any time special ™

Look us up on-line at: http://www.romance.net   HIAMA2

HARLEQUIN®

I N T R I G U E®

COMING NEXT MONTH

#521 FATHER, LOVER, BODYGUARD by Cassie Miles
Captive Hearts
Amanda Fielding remembered nothing of the robbery or blow to the head that caused her partial amnesia. When she woke in the hospital, she gazed into the dark, sexy eyes of Dr. David Haines—her former lover. David swore to protect her from the danger stalking her—and she knew she'd finally have to tell him about their baby...

#522 WANTED: COWBOY by Kelsey Roberts
The Rose Tattoo
Barbara Prather ranted on about Cade Landry, her cowboy protector—but she couldn't seem to get enough of him! As the only witness to a murder, Barbara had an assassin on her trail. Cade kidnapped her to save her life—but was his interest professional...or personal?

#523 HER EYEWITNESS by Rita Herron
Blinded in the line of duty, police officer Collin Cash had a transplant to regain his sight—and woke to a vision of murder. The dead man's widow stood accused—and only Collin could prove her innocence. When Sydney Green discovered Collin's identity, would she accept his help...and his heart?

#524 THE BRIDE'S SECRET by Adrianne Lee
Nikki Navarro would do anything to find the family she'd never known—even take on Chris Conrad, the dark and sexy owner of Wedding House. Nikki was the spitting image of the bride whose portrait graced the master suite—and only Chris could protect her from someone determined she would never know if she was, in fact, the bride's secret...

Look us up on-line at: http://www.romance.net

HARLEQUIN · CELEBRATES

FIVE DECADES OF ROMANCE

In July 1999 Harlequin Superromance®
brings you *The Lyon Legacy*—a
brand-new 3-in-1 book from popular
authors Peg Sutherland, Roz Denny Fox
& Ruth Jean Dale

3 stories for the price of 1!

Join us as we celebrate
Harlequin's 50th Anniversary!

Look for these other
Harlequin Superromance®
titles wherever books are sold July 1999:

A COP'S GOOD NAME (#846)
by Linda Markowiak
THE MAN FROM HIGH MOUNTAIN (#848)
by Kay David
HER OWN RANGER (#849)
by Anne Marie Duquette
SAFE HAVEN (#850)
by Evelyn A. Crowe
JESSIE'S FATHER (#851)
by C. J. Carmichael